ELLY REDDING was born in London but now lives in Bedfordshire with her hu~~~ ~~~ Having originally written screenplays, her first novel '~ Festival of Romance's New Talent Av and watching the waves, alt

True
Colours

Elly Redding

SilverWood

Published in 2016 by SilverWood Books
SilverWood Books Ltd

14 Small Street, Bristol, BS1 1DE, United Kingdom
www.silverwoodbooks.co.uk

ISBN 978-1-78132-554-4 (paperback)
ISBN 978-1-78132-555-1 (ebook)

British Library Cataloguing in Publication Data
A CIP catalogue record for this book is available from
the British Library

Page design and typesetting by SilverWood Books
Printed on responsibly sourced paper

To all those who shared my dream, thank you for everything

Chapter 1

As she stubbed her toe on the edge of her cast iron bath, Kate had a feeling today was not going to go according to plan. Spilling marmalade on the cuff of her favourite silk blouse at breakfast did nothing to lessen this feeling of unease. But nothing, absolutely nothing, could have prepared her for what was waiting for her at the office.

"Hi," greeted Lydia. "Perfect timing. I've got your ex on the phone."

"My ex what?" Kate hobbled over to her desk, trying to extricate her arms from the lining of her jacket.

"How many ex-fiancés do you have?"

"Ah...*that* ex." She meant Saul. There was no-one else. How could there be? No other man had ever swept her off her feet and offered her the world. Nor declared, on bended knee, in front of all their friends, that their love would last forever.

She threw the jacket defiantly over the back of the chair.

And no other man, only a month away from their wedding, had been discovered in his London art gallery with his assistant, who looked as though she was in the middle of a game of strip poker. *That* ex-fiancé. Her heart gave a treacherous lurch, although she couldn't imagine why.

"Tell him I'm out...that I'm on another call...that I'm too busy." Kate paused, kicking off her shoe to relieve her swollen toe. "And then ask him how the hell he got my phone number."

"Are you sure you wouldn't rather ask him yourself?"

"Me – speak to him? I'd rather burn in hell first."

"I'll take that as a 'no', shall I?"

Kate nodded emphatically, before diving under her desk to relocate her shoe. When she reappeared, Lydia was looking at her apologetically.

"I think he may have heard all of that," she mouthed, indicating the mute button, which was anything but on mute. "Sorry." Picking up the receiver with the precision of someone about to defuse a time bomb, she held it to her ear and listened.

"He says he got your number from the website, and it's good to know you still think so highly of him..."

That wasn't quite how Kate would have described it.

"...and that, if it makes you feel any better, he'd rather not speak to you either, but as he's just passing by and needs to see you..."

"See me? What does he mean by that – by the word 'see'?"

"I don't know, shall I ask?" Lydia enquired, a smile hovering in the wings. "Saul, what did you mean by... Oh, I see, you heard that too. Yes. Yes. One moment please." Turning back to Kate, she explained, "Apparently he needs to see you about a wedding."

Now Kate *knew* she should have stayed in bed this morning. Wedding, what wedding? Surely he wasn't going to invite her to his? No. Not even Saul in his most demonic moments would be that unkind. Or would he? And what did he mean by 'just passing'? Saul was never *just* passing. He was either passing or not passing. There was never anything *just* about anything he ever did.

"Whose..." Kate opened her mouth, but the words wouldn't come. All she could do was sit and stare at Lydia, and wonder whether she would ever be able to speak again.

"Shall I tell him he can come then?"

To Kate's relief, the muscles in her neck still worked perfectly.

"I'll assume that that's another no, shall I?" Lydia put the receiver back to her ear. "Saul, I'm afraid... Oh!"

"Oh what?" Kate managed to gasp, fumbling in her drawer for her inhaler.

"Oh, he appears to have gone, which I can only assume means he's on his way up here."

"Oh, no, he's not." And then, as though she'd just been zapped with a defibrillator, Kate sprang into action. "God, look at me! He can't come up here. I didn't even have time to do anything with my hair this morning." She pulled out a little mirror from a side drawer, and panicked at the reflection as a mass of shiny black waves fell in all directions over her shoulders. "Oh, Lydia, why can't the glass ever lie? And I've still got marmalade on my blouse. I look like a freak. He'll think I've gone to pot since that...that... I can't let him see me."

Frantically shoving her shoe on over her bruised toe, Kate hobbled across towards the window. Cautiously, she drew back the blind and peeped outside at the street below.

"Oh my God, he's here," she groaned, turning back in desperation. "Lydia? He mustn't see me. Can't you just beam me up somewhere? I'm not fussy. I'll go anywhere, just so long as

9

I don't have to share it with him. Please?"

"The ladies' cloakroom. That's it. Go upstairs and you can hide in there until he's gone."

"I'm not hiding in the loo. Not after last Christmas. They already think I'm some sort of pervert, those people on the top floor."

"Only because they caught you getting changed in there for that fancy dress do," Lydia chuckled, her blue eyes sparkling at the memory.

"How was I to know that my very clear request for a Cinderella costume would be transformed into something from the living dead?"

"Slipknot, to be precise. Although I have to say I think you looked even more menacing than the rock group themselves!"

"Well, I'm glad you found it so amusing. For weeks afterwards, I kept having nightmares that I'd wake up and find myself on YouTube."

From the other side of their second-floor office, the front door buzzer sounded.

"He's here," Lydia hissed. "Now go. Just keep away from any more masks. I'll let him in and I'll come upstairs and get you when the coast is clear, OK?"

"What will you say to him?"

"I'll tell him the truth: that you hate his guts so much that you had to rush to the loo."

"Lydia!"

"OK, OK, perhaps a bit dramatic, but don't worry, I'll think of something. Now *go!*"

*

If Saul had thought his life was spinning dangerously out of control three years ago, when he'd first met Kate, today it was heading for a distant galaxy. It had been from the moment he'd agreed to this crazy outing to Wimbledon. And now, as he removed his finger from the buzzer, there was nothing he could do to pull it back from the outer reaches. Nothing, that was, except walk away.

He stared up at the office block, six floors hideously cased in concrete. Overhead, rain clouds hovered ominously. It was April. Minutes earlier the sky had been a textbook blue but Saul preferred the grey; it matched his mood perfectly.

He took a step back and sank his hands deep into the trouser pockets of a suit from Savile Row. He would give Kate five minutes and then he'd go. He would not press that buzzer again. He would not give her the satisfaction of keeping him waiting. No-one kept him waiting. It was not the way he did business.

But then he didn't usually pay social calls to women where he knew his presence would be unwelcome. Women who would prefer to see him six feet under rather than in excellent health on their doorstep.

He paused. Why had he used the plural? There was only one woman who qualified for that description. Only one woman he'd allowed to get that close. And that had been a mistake. A huge mistake, and not one he'd be making again. Affairs of the heart were not for him. His life might be verging on the monastic, as his sister, Maria, had so delicately put it, but at least it was free from the pitfalls of youthful exuberance.

11

Saul slipped his right hand out from his pocket and pressed the buzzer again.

Oh yes, as far as he was concerned, he'd tried love once. And in his opinion, it was vastly overrated.

Kate collapsed on to the stool in the ladies' cloakroom. She was finding it difficult to breathe and she knew exactly who to blame. Diving into her handbag, she produced her inhaler and gave herself two quick puffs.

What did he think he was doing, invading her personal space? She'd worked hard to build this wall around herself, and the last thing she wanted, or needed, was for some jumped up ex-fiancé to arrive with his trumpet and knock it down again. She and Lydia were partners in a very successful translation business, which they'd established just over two years ago, and she didn't want Saul poking his nose into that. She didn't want him rummaging around in any part of her life, let alone her office, making suggestions for improvements. If he wanted to play corporate games, he could go back to running his own entities, an art gallery off Piccadilly, or his original company, Preston Aviation, one of the largest private aircraft leasing companies in the country.

Although hell would normally be Kate's first, and preferred, choice of destination for her ex-fiancé, at this stage she wasn't so particular. Anywhere would do, just so long as it wasn't here and with her.

The only problem was that Saul didn't appear to be aware of this. Only minutes after he'd arrived, Kate could hear the door to their office open and close again. Instead of going back down the stairs, though, the footsteps were coming in her direction. Strong, masculine footsteps, getting closer and closer, sending her heart and imagination into overdrive. What if Saul had prised the truth out of Lydia? What if he were to fling open that door, and find her cowering in a cloakroom? Where the plumbing leaked and tiles fell from the walls along with the cobwebs?

In desperation, she glanced up at the small window over the washbasin. Not if she could help it, he wasn't. She glanced back at the size ten reflection in the mirror. Body – window? Window – body? Were the two compatible? And if so, what were the chances of success when she reached the other side? Would there be a conveniently situated ladder? A soft-topped lorry? Or even a ledge to stand on?

"Kate?"

And did she care?

"I know you're in there." The voice was unmistakable.

"Go away," she shouted, frantically reassessing her options.

"I don't really think you're in a position to make demands, do you, trapped as you are? Unless, of course, you're thinking of taking up abseiling. In which case, may I advise restraint? You're on the fourth floor. You're afraid of heights and I'm not standing in the right place to catch you."

Good. It would ruin the whole point of the exercise if he were. She didn't tell him that though. Instead she suggested he make an appointment; that if he wanted to see her, he should do what everyone else did.

"But I'm not everyone else, am I? I'm the guy who's still considering suing you for breach of contract."

13

"Contract – what contract?"

"Your promise to marry me."

"You bastard." It was the first thing she could think of to say, but she thought it summed up the situation perfectly. "In which case, may I suggest you contact my lawyer? I think you'll find I've a very strong case for a counterclaim. Or has something conveniently slipped your memory? Let me give you a clue. She had an amazing pair of breasts."

"If you're referring to Claudia—"

"See. You do remember."

She could hear Saul take a deep breath. "I'm not going into this again, Kate," he stated in a voice that left her in no doubt as to her position on his Christmas list. "I tried to explain to you what happened at the time, but you refused to listen to me. That was your prerogative. Mine is not having to repeat myself. Now, are you going to come out and face me like a...a..."

"An ex-fiancée?"

"...or not?"

Kate thought about it for a nanosecond. "Not."

"Right then." There was a brief pause, during which Kate steeled herself for the inevitable. "You do realise that there's nothing to stop me from ignoring the dress code and coming straight in?" He must be referring to the picture on the door, a woman in a crinoline, hanging at forty-five degrees. "And that you could do nothing to stop me if I so chose?"

She nodded.

"I'll take your silence as an affirmative."

He could take it any way he wanted. Just so long as he stayed where he was. But he wouldn't. Saul never did anything he didn't want to and Kate knew that better than anyone. Any second now the handle would turn and he would appear. She would be illuminated by enough lighting to rival the National Grid, her imperfections magnified to dinosaur proportions.

Kate shuddered. It was not an attractive proposition, which meant there was only one thing for it. She would have to give herself up, hope he'd grown incredibly short-sighted during the last few years, and that his glasses were in his other jacket. And she would have to do it now, before it was too late.

"Saul..." she began, but then she stopped. She could hear footsteps, yet they weren't hers. They were his. And they weren't coming towards her. They were going away. Back down the stairs. He was leaving. She crept towards the door and opened it, cautiously. She could hear voices. A rich, resonant voice followed by such gentle, bird-like chatter. They were talking, Saul and Lydia. They were laughing, enjoying each other's company.

Suddenly it took all her strength not to fling back the door and join them.

Saul sank down into the driver's seat of his Maserati. He was shaking. God damn it, his hands were actually shaking. He glanced through the window, back up at the building. And he hadn't even seen her; at least not face to face. Yet she'd been there, with him, from the moment he'd stepped into her office. Her choice of furnishing, of pictures, of colour – it was all there, just as it was when they'd been together.

And he could smell her too, that pleasing aroma of perfume,

leading him to where he knew she was hiding. He didn't need Lydia to tell him what she was up to. Or try and pretend she wasn't there, that she'd had to dash out to see a sick relative, because he knew that wasn't true. He'd seen Kate at the window, just a few minutes earlier. And by God he wasn't going to leave until she'd seen him too.

He didn't know why it was suddenly so important, when he'd told himself it wasn't. Or why, when he knew she was about to crack, he'd moved away. He'd like to think it was chivalry, that he didn't wish to foist his presence on someone who still so obviously didn't wish to receive it, but it wasn't that simple. If it had been, he would have left the invitation with Lydia in the first place.

No. It was far more complex than that. So complex, in fact, that a lesser man might have given in and sought professional help. But Saul didn't need professional help. Despite his earlier protestations, he knew exactly why he'd allowed himself to be talked into this meeting. Why he'd bounded up the stairs to try and see her. And why he was still sitting outside her office.

The only question, as he hit the ignition button, was what the hell was he going to do about it?

Lydia waited until the Maserati had finally driven off before putting her head around the cloakroom door. "It's OK, you coward, he's gone."

"Et tu, Brute?"

But Lydia wasn't listening. "Oh, I know he's the enemy," she said, her blue eyes glazing over, "but you've got to admit, he's one hell of a hunk."

Kate couldn't believe her ears. "After everything I've told you?"

It was bad enough her mother still insisting that the man walked on water, but now her closest friend? "Lydia, how could you? And how could you tell him where I was?"

"I didn't. Honest. He just seemed to sort of know."

That didn't surprise Kate. Nothing about him ever had. "So what did he want?"

Lydia passed her a gold envelope, scrawled with a fine black italic script. "His sister's getting married. Apparently, she really wants you to come. She didn't want to contact you herself – she thought you'd refuse, because of *you know who*. So she managed to persuade *you know who* to come round and give you the invitation in person, and to tell you that if you could overcome your prejudices—"

Kate's eyebrows shot up. "My what?"

"Prejudices – his words, not mine – if you could see your way to overcoming these 'prejudices', he knew it would mean a great deal to Maria if you came."

So it was his sister who was getting married, and not him. His dear, sweet sister who was walking down the aisle. And suddenly Kate's whole body felt like jelly, although she couldn't understand why. Why, after years of successful propaganda, it should choose now to follow some secret agenda all of its own.

"Did…did he say anything else?"

"He asked how you were, when you weren't barricading yourself in cloakrooms."

"He did?"

"And…"

Kate held her breath. "And?"

"And I'm truly sorry about this…"

17

A warning bell sounded somewhere in Kate's mind. "Sorry about what?"

"He asked whether you had a diary. And I said yes. And then," Lydia added, concentrating on twirling a piece of plaster around the end of her finger, "he asked in that voice which is impossible to refuse, you know the one..."

Oh, yes, Kate knew only too well: the one that wrapped around your heart like a velvet shawl and robbed you of the power of independent thought. "So you opened up my Outlook and, guess what, there was a large empty space on the day of the wedding?"

Lydia nodded guiltily. "There was also something else which caught his eye. A trip to the theatre with Tim, next Saturday. And...and he asked who Tim was."

"Oh, Lydia, please tell me you didn't say my employee. Please?" Kate beseeched, feeling the nightmare take an unexpected twist.

"Give me some credit. Of course, I didn't. I said, with a sort of coy expression on my face, 'Tim? Oh, he's a dear friend of Kate's.'"

Kate was overcome with a sudden surge of elation. From the pits of despair had come an unexpected triumph. She had a surrogate boyfriend. Tim might have long ginger hair that looked as though he lived in a permanent state of fright, the beginnings of a beer belly and an earring through both ears, but for the moment none of that mattered. He was a really nice guy. And Saul thought he was her boyfriend, that she'd found happiness with somebody else. Maybe today wasn't such a disaster after all.

Chapter 2

"Why don't you take Tim?" Lydia asked. "The invitation says *plus one*. Saul already thinks you two are an item, so why don't you ask him?"

Two months later, Kate almost wished she had. She almost wished she'd declined the invitation, too, but it was a little late for that. She'd said yes. She'd looked into the face of her future and told herself she could handle it. That she was doing this for Maria, the sister-in-law she'd very nearly had.

Only now, as the day of the wedding finally dawned, Kate wasn't so sure. She was experiencing a bout of nerves to rival those of a bride. Whatever had possessed her to think she could get away with this – that she could meet Saul, face to face, without feeling the need to trampoline out of the nearest window? She couldn't. It was going to be a disaster. Another catastrophe to add to the long list of mishaps which only seemed to happen when she fell in love.

She glanced across at her reflection in the hall mirror. Well, at least that was one scenario she didn't need to worry about today. She might have lost weight since their break-up, but she'd not lost her mind. Nor had she lost her curves. They were a little smaller, granted, but they were still there. And as for today she'd decided to wear a snugly fitting little black dress, over which she'd fling an emerald satin jacket, Kate was extremely grateful.

With her mass of jet black curls scooped up into a half-bun, leaving wisps of fine, silky waves to fall becomingly on to her shoulders, she was power dressing and she knew it, but without a hand to hold, or a shoulder to lean on, she was going to need all the support she could get.

Once inside the registry office in Tunbridge Wells, Kate tried to focus on the small circle immediately surrounding her. To her relief there was no-one she recognised, at least not yet, which was just the way she liked it. No awkward questions. No awkward silences. She risked a glance a little further afield. No awkward reminders of anything.

And then someone asked the guests to move out of the corridor and into the room. It was on the tip of Kate's tongue to say no. To insist she was perfectly happy where she was, when she realised she was in the minority, and that she had no option but to go along with it. To allow herself to be swept up in a tidal wave of obedience.

Bodies buffeted against each other, until she finally came to rest only a few feet away from the one person she did recognise. A man so tall and powerful that it was all she could do not to ask for a stepladder. But Kate didn't want to look Saul in the eye. She didn't want to look at him anywhere. She turned round and tried to push back the way she'd come, but she couldn't. Right of passage was one way and one way only. She had no choice but to turn back and face him.

He was staring down at her. Those dark eyes demanding a response, some acknowledgement of his presence, but she couldn't give him one. The expression on her face was fixed, fashioned for occasions such as these. If she shifted it just a fraction, then she might as well throw it away all together.

And so she watched in silence as he resumed his conversation with the bespectacled and portly gentleman beside him; as the blonde to his right continued to coil herself around Saul's anatomy. She watched and she wondered. Why did Lydia have to be right? Why was he still a hunk? (She hated the word, but it did sum up his physique beautifully.)

And who was the woman beside him – his latest girlfriend? And if so, since when had he started to go for women with the limb capacity of an octopus? With extremities so long and slim that, if they weren't bobbing along at the bottom of the ocean, they could be found wrapped around ex-fiancés?

She turned away. She was feeling breathless. Serves you right, she told herself, delving into her handbag for an inhaler, for being so unkind. She's probably a perfectly charming person, with a Masters from Cambridge and a string of qualifications as long as your arm. Or longer. After all, is it her fault she seems to find Saul so attractive? Wasn't that exactly what you did once? Kate cursed silently, trying to push her way back through the crowd. Before he let you down? Before…

She stopped. She was getting nowhere. She was still surrounded by people, crowds of people, and none of them were paying her any attention. No-one was moving out of her way. She could feel her chest tighten; her breathing becoming more and more laboured.

A wave of mounting panic swept over her. She had to get out of here. She just had to. She wasn't having an asthma attack. Not here. Not in front of Saul. Not in front of the one man whose hand had just come out of nowhere and landed on her shoulder.

"Are you all right?" he asked, pulling her round to face him.

"Fine," she managed to gasp. It was a lie. She was slowly suffocating, but she wasn't going to let him know that. She didn't need his help, she needed…

"You've not taken your inhaler, have you?"

…to have someone tell her something she didn't already know. She shook her head.

"Then for God's sake, Kate, take it."

She was too exhausted to argue. Besides, to argue you needed to be able to speak and she'd lost that ability several minutes ago. So she did as instructed and gave herself two puffs.

"Better?"

She nodded. It was another lie but she had to do something. She couldn't bear to have him look at her like that, so intently, as though he might actually care.

"Please…" she began, but she never finished. He'd grabbed hold of her shoulders and was cutting through the crowd of people with her in front of him, like a scythe through corn.

In other circumstances she would have fought like a cat to get him to release her, but feline activity involved energy and she didn't have any. She couldn't even raise a squeal, let alone a claw. And so she did what she swore she would never do again. She relaxed back against his shoulders, such firm and muscular shoulders, and allowed him to steer her out into the corridor.

"Now," Saul said, lowering her down carefully on to a seat, that the attendant had quickly provided, "before you embark on a tirade against me for daring to touch you, I suggest you master breathing." She was still fighting for air, her chest battling to expel the carbon dioxide, as he crouched down beside her. "Let me look at your puffer."

She held out her hand to reveal the small blue object.

He snatched it from her. "No wonder it's not working," he said, shaking it. "It's almost empty. Where's your spare?"

It was at this point Kate wanted to scream, to tell him to go away and leave her to die with dignity. Anything was better than this, than having him look down at her with such exasperation in those dark eyes. But she couldn't. Her lungs were begging for oxygen. So she passed him her bag, praying not only that the spare was in there, but that he wouldn't make fun of the other contents.

After their break-up, Lydia had been so concerned that Kate, in a fit of pique, would embark on an orgy with the entire male race, that she'd insisted she always carry a condom. She'd even slipped some into nearly every bag Kate possessed. And that was where they'd stayed. Of course, if Saul examined them too closely, he would also notice that their expiry date had probably passed, but that wouldn't stop him having a good laugh at her expense.

"Now," he said, pulling out the inhaler and shaking it, "take it. At least twice."

As slowly as she could, Kate breathed out. Placing the puffer into her mouth, she pressed and tried to breathe in. She repeated the process several times and began to feel the difference. At last she was regaining control of her destiny. At last people would stop staring at them.

She glanced up at Saul, watching as he sprang back up on to his feet and, stepping back, readjusted the cuffs of his grey suit jacket. Why did he have to look so distinguished? Why, during those last few years, couldn't he have metamorphosed into a frog instead of remaining a prince? Apart from a few grey hairs around his once-dark temples, and a slight furrowing of his forehead, little had changed. They were still the same harshly crafted features that once she'd loved. That, under her gaze, had gradually mellowed to reveal the man behind the mask.

Kate sighed. Once, that was, a long time ago. Now they were all levelled at her with an exasperation she knew only too well.

"You'll never learn, will you?"

"Sorry?"

"Asthma. It's not a game."

"I…know."

"It could kill you."

"Thanks," she puffed, "for…reminding…me."

"I shouldn't have to. For Christ's sake, Kate," he broke off and ran his fingers through his hair, "what did you think you were playing at back there? Don't you—"

But he never finished. An official had tapped him on the shoulder and was whispering something equally important in his ear.

"I've got to go," Saul said suddenly. It was as though the last few minutes had never occurred, as though they were strangers. Two strangers who, once, a long time ago, had nearly shared a lifetime together. He cleared his throat. "If you're feeling all right…"

Kate made herself nod a response.

"Then perhaps I'll see you later?"

But before she could answer, before she could tell him she thought it highly unlikely, he was gone. She was by herself, once again.

Chapter 3

Saul drained the last dregs of wine from his glass and looked across to where Kate was dancing. Why had Maria insisted on asking her? What had possessed her to accept? And why, oh why, did she have to look so goddamned wonderful? A little thinner, maybe, but still bloody sexy.

He watched as she melted into the music, glancing up every so often to smile at her partner. Who the hell was he? Some Adonis from Greek mythology? Saul began to play with the stem of his glass, aware he'd drunk more of the Shiraz than he'd intended, and that it was having the opposite effect to the one he'd hoped for.

It had been a hell of a shock seeing her again. All his plans of keeping his distance had been stripped from him the moment he'd noticed her fumble in her handbag for what he knew would be her inhaler. Tough, decisive, indestructible she might be on the surface, but when she had an attack there was no-one in the room more vulnerable. And when she'd looked up at him with those large green eyes, he knew he had to move, to put some distance between them, before he made an even bigger fool of himself.

The golden boy whispered something in her ear. Saul watched

as she responded with a little giggle. As she tossed her head back, and a trickle of shiny black hair escaped down the nape of her neck. That beautiful expanse of flesh, smooth, silky flesh that once he'd kissed, that once…

He stopped. What the hell did he think he was doing? This was not how it should be. He was supposed to be entertaining Patti. He glanced across at where Maria had decided to place her: a suitable distance away from her brother. And she was probably right. Not, on reflection, his best choice, but it was a little too late to go back on it now.

Patti, at least, was enjoying herself, so his conscience was clear; her laughter cut swathes across the tables. Strange how that noise grated on him. There was no warmth in it, no sincerity, no infectious giggle. Not like Kate's. His Kate's. Her eyes would light up when she talked to you. When she found something amusing, they would sparkle like newly cut jewels, radiating exquisite pleasure from every finely-drawn feature on that pale face.

How do I love thee? Let me count the ways.
I love thee to the depth and breadth and height
My soul can reach…

Saul broke off. Now he knew he was in trouble. He was quoting bloody poetry. In a desperate attempt to quell the fire raging within, he pulled a bottle of mineral water towards him. Finding a clean glass to his left, he poured himself a generous dose and sat back, waiting for the flames to subside.

*

Kate could sense she was being watched. That the one person she was doing her very best to ignore wasn't ignoring her. And she knew she'd made a mistake, a very silly mistake. That she should have used the asthma as an excuse and driven back to London while she still could, rather than face the family home in Kent.

Instead she'd ignored every instinct for survival, and had found herself following the crowd, through the beams and bustle of an Elizabethan farmhouse, and out again into the same garden in which she and Saul had held their own engagement party. The pungent fragrance of roses wafting around her, music and laughter filling the air, just as they had back then, on that warm summer's evening in June.

The marquee, in shades of white and pastel pink, the canvas billowing in the breeze, drawing her back to a time she'd tried so hard to forget. When she was the star, plucked out of obscurity, and allowed to sparkle centre stage, while all around congratulations showered down on her, like confetti at a wedding. A wedding that was never to be.

Memories…

Kate blinked hard against the penetrating glare of the sun.

…of how Saul had whipped a red rose from a vase and, against the slow and husky strains of *Je t'aime*, had bent down on one knee and declared his undying love for her. And how, shielded from the rest of the party by a tune that played only for them, she'd leant towards him and raised the petals tenderly to her lips to caress their smooth, satin tips.

She shivered.

But roses fade and wilt…

"Caterina?"

…and some things are never meant to be.

"*Ciao, mia cara, come stai?*"

"Luisa?" Kate came hurtling back to reality with a bump. "*Bene*," she gasped as a beautifully defined Italian woman grabbed hold of her arms and kissed her enthusiastically on both cheeks. "*Grazie.*"

"Of course you're not all right." Saul's mother said dismissively. "How can you be? You're all alone. Saul?" She addressed the man on her right, who was happily discussing the latest thing in rock with a heavily studded niece on his father's side. "Why didn't you bring Kate? You go off and play the conquering hero at the registry office and then what do you do? Go and leave the poor child to fend for herself. What type of impression does that give?"

His expression said it all. But before he could add words to the look of sheer incredulity, Luisa had returned to the task of welcoming her guest. "You must come and see me. I've so missed our little chats. You mustn't be a stranger. Tell her, Saul, she mustn't be a stranger!"

Kate caught his eye. He would have sent anyone else halfway to the moon by now with very little chance of a return trip, but not his mother. Not his family. Not anyone he really cared about. They were sacrosanct, which neatly ruled Kate out.

"How are you feeling?" he asked.

Luisa raised her arms in despair. "Is that all you can say?" she cried. "After all this time? You're such a stuffed shirt – just like your father." She quickly made the sign of the cross. "God rest his soul." But before Saul could put in a word for himself, his father, or even his shirt, her attention had wandered away towards the next guest, an over-enthusiastic cousin, Kate remembered, from the heel of Italy, who was carrying a rolled-up umbrella and answered to the name of Vinny.

She bit her bottom lip. "Mothers," she replied, trying not to smile, nor examine Saul's chest too closely. "Always think they know best."

He followed her line of vision. "It's not stuffed," he said quietly.

"Sorry?" Kate raised her eyes.

"The shirt," he added helpfully.

"Oh. That."

"Yes, that. By the way, how's yours?"

Now Kate was even more confused. "My what?"

"Mother?"

"Oh." At last they were on safe ground. Neutral ground. Or at least they would have been with anyone else but Helen. "You know her." Unfortunately for Kate, Saul did, only too well. "No doubt she'll be on the phone first thing tomorrow morning, expecting a detailed report."

His eyes narrowed. "And what will you tell her?"

"So far? Saw Maria get married. Came to reception. And…"

"And?"

"…and went home."

Saul looked almost rueful. "That won't satisfy Helen," he said, his deep voice telling her what she already knew.

"I know. But I haven't come here to satisfy my mother."

"Then who have you come here to satisfy?"

But before she could answer that, before she could even begin to think of a response, Saul's sister came to her rescue.

"You came!" Maria exclaimed, hugging Kate affectionately. "I'm so, so glad." She was beaming at her with the radiance that only a bride could generate, looking more like a medieval princess than a dentist; the simple lines of her cream and gold satin dress flowing away from her curvaceous hips and on to the floor below. Her dark hair was embroidered with flowers of matching colours, with just a hint of greenery.

"You look wonderful," Kate declared. "And I hope you'll both be very happy," she added with a glance at the proud groom: a chubby, balding stockbroker from Surrey.

"We will," Maria assured her before taking her to one side. "I know you must have had your reasons for leaving him, and I know it's none of my business, but please don't judge Saul too harshly. He's a good man, even if he is my brother."

That was the last thing Kate wanted to hear. Not today of all days. It would force her to remember, and she didn't want to. She didn't want to remember how close she'd come to spending the rest of her life with him.

Or how, one sultry August evening, having ruined everything, he'd sat by her bed in hospital as she'd had one of the worst asthma attacks ever. She didn't want to remember that, or how she'd puffed at him to go away. And with a look that had broken her heart, he'd done just that.

Memories. Kate wiped a tear from the corner of her eye and made herself enter the marquee. In front of her lay white damask tablecloths, adorned with pink and white displays of freshly cut flowers, polished silver and sparkling glasses. No expense had been

31

spared. She glanced up at the seating arrangements, and hoped that Saul's generosity had extended to her placement. That she wouldn't find herself sitting next to someone with the personality of a zombie or the wit of a slug.

And she was in luck. On her right, an ex-test pilot enthralled her with tales of a world where men were heroes. And on her left was Dan, a university lecturer who looked as though he'd walked off an American film set. Not only that, but he could dance. Slowly at first; he didn't want to exhaust her – he'd seen what had happened at the registry office (was there anyone who hadn't, Kate wondered?) – but as her lungs responded to the challenge, he asked her for another dance.

And then another.

And then, just as Kate was beginning to relax and forget she was being watched by a pair of distinctly disturbing eyes, she felt someone tap her on the shoulder.

"May I?" enquired a voice from her past.

"No." She swung round to face Saul, not quite able to believe the audacity of the man. "I don't wish to dance with you. Go and ask your...your octopus. I'm perfectly happy with..." She turned back to seek the same reassurance from Dan, but, to her horror, he'd gone.

"Looks like you don't have any choice," Saul said, gripping Kate firmly by the wrists and pulling her towards him. "Besides, my octopus, as you so beautifully put it, is busy."

"Lucky her," Kate murmured. Then, stretching her neck back so she could give him the full benefit of her thoughts, she added, "You have just ruined what was promising to be a very interesting evening."

"And there was I thinking you needed rescuing. Or did I misread those glances in my direction? Look," he added quickly, before Kate could disillusion him, "we used to be good on the dance floor, if I remember correctly. Let's show them how it's done, if only for old times' sake. Just one dance. Then you can go back and continue enjoying your evening. Without me."

And to her surprise, Kate couldn't refuse. She knew she should. That she should reject him there and then, in front of everyone, and make him realise that she was not something he could pick up and put down when the mood suited. That when she'd said it was over, three years ago, she'd meant it, every single word of it, but she couldn't.

The chords of *Temptation* were reverberating around the canvas. Its powerful beat increasing the tempo and filling the floor with so much music and movement, she just knew she had to be part of it, even if it did mean sharing it with Saul. The one man who definitely wasn't on her dance-card!

So, throwing caution to the wind, Kate allowed him to guide her, to take her by the hand and find a space amongst the other dancers. She knew people were taking an interest again, but she didn't care. After all, it was just one song. What was the danger in that?

In feeling the warmth of his skin against hers, the strength of those hands as he drew her towards him and then spun her away? In knowing that every time she brushed against his chest, she wanted to stay there, to feel the beat of his heart? Just one dance, he'd said, for old times' sake, and then it would all be over.

And then, before Kate could catch her breath, it was. She stole a glance at Saul. She needed him to release her and to let her go, but still he held her hand, her pale, cold hand, tightly within his. The band was playing *Je t'aime*. All around, dancers were sliding into one another's arms.

"Do you remember?" he asked.

She nodded. "But I was young then. Young and innocent."

"And now?"

"Now I know better."

He drew her firmly towards him. "Dance with me." It was as though she hadn't spoken. As though he was in a world of his own. And as his arms, those strong, protective arms, folded around her, and she felt his breath, warm and gentle, against her forehead, Kate found herself tumbling back into that world, to a time she was trying so hard to forget.

"Saul?" She tried to arch her neck back, to tilt her face up towards his. "This…this isn't a good idea." Looking straight into his eyes, she realised for the first time that they were slightly bloodshot. "You'll wake up tomorrow morning and regret this."

"No, I won't, my love. If I'd stayed over there and watched you, or come over here and thumped the living daylights out of your golden Adonis, then yes, I might have regretted it. But being here, dancing with you, just touching you, feeling you next to me, this I don't regret."

"You will. Besides, this is madness." She tried to disentangle herself with her elbows. "If you would just excuse me…"

But he wouldn't. He was studying her mouth in such a way that Kate knew immediately what he was thinking.

"Saul?" And she was right. Within seconds he'd silenced all dissension, his lips sending her heart into such chaos that for a while

34

it lost the plot altogether as it fluctuated wildly between protestation and pleasure, her brain ranting at her to resist, while her soul screamed that resistance against such determination was futile.

She was right. This was madness, but it was such a sweet madness. A madness that made her wonder why they'd ever separated. Why she'd spent the last three years telling herself time and time again that she hated him, that their love had been a mistake.

A madness lasting for just a moment; sanity soon prevailed, bringing with it a latent anger, that gave her the power to push, to try and prise herself away from him.

Saul released her almost immediately. "Kate... Christ, I..." He stepped back, his hands raking through his hair. "I don't know why..."

But Kate didn't say anything. She couldn't. She knew if she opened her mouth, still tingling from the ecstasy of that kiss, nothing would happen. There were no words to describe what had just taken place. No words to describe the tumult of emotions that were flooding her senses. And even if there were, now was not the time to voice them. Not unless she wanted to be carted off, ranting and raving, to the nearest padded cell. Later, when she was back in her flat, she would try and make some sense of it all. That was the time for emotion, but not here, not now.

Aware that they were not alone, that everyone was watching them, Kate turned away. Moving back across the dance floor, with guests springing to either side, as though she were Moses at the parting of the Red Sea, she quickly gathered up her handbag and jacket from her chair.

She didn't have the courage to face Maria or Saul's mother,

and Dan was nowhere to be seen. But it didn't matter. Nothing mattered anymore. It was over. Her ordeal was finally over. And, as she reached the welcoming gap in the canvas and felt the cool night air fall against her crimson cheeks, Kate knew she really should be glad.

Chapter 4

Sleep was impossible. How could she sleep? She couldn't even stand still, let alone lie down. What had Saul thought he was doing? It was one thing to ask her to dance. That Kate could understand – just – but to kiss her, there, in front of everyone? That would take a little more explaining, if only she knew where to begin.

By the time her mother phoned the following morning, Kate had given up. It was very simple. There were no explanations. At least none she liked. And she'd neither the willpower nor the energy to pursue it further. All she wanted to do was forget it had ever happened, which – unfortunately for Kate – was the last thing on her mother's mind.

"Well?" Helen asked.

Kate threw the sheet over her head and collapsed back against the pillows. The inquisition had begun. "Well what?" she groaned from her new hiding place.

"How did it go?"

"Can I phone you back?"

"Why? Don't tell me you've got someone there? Kate? Answer me. You've not embarked on one of those one-night stands, have you? You never know where they've been these days. I do hope you took precautions. Tell your poor mother you've at least done that?"

"Yes, Mother. I mean, no, Mother, I haven't. It wasn't necessary, I—"

"Now, of course," Helen cut in, "if it were Saul, then that would be an entirely different matter. Is it Saul?"

"No!" Kate flung the sheet from her and sat bolt upright. "Would you just let me get a word in edgeways? It's nothing like that. I'm here in this flat, by myself. Do you hear me? *By myself.*"

There was a long silence at the other end, followed by an exaggerated sniff and a "Well, of course, if you don't want to talk about it…" at which point Kate jumped out of bed. Her mother was right. She didn't want to talk about it. It was eight o'clock in the morning. She'd had less than three hours' sleep. And she needed caffeine, but she knew there would be no peace until she did talk to her mother and so she bowed to the inevitable.

"What do you want to know?"

"Everything, my dear. I want to hear everything."

Five minutes later and Kate was thinking of changing career. So masterful was her fabrication of the last twenty-four hours that she felt sure stardom beckoned.

Unfortunately, her mother seemed less impressed. "And?" Helen prompted.

"And what?"

"Oh, Katherine. I'm your mother. I gave birth to you. Twenty-four hours of agonising labour. Do you think I don't know you? Well, let me tell you something. I went to visit Mrs Smythe yesterday. Do you remember her? You were at school with Lucy."

Kate remembered. How could she forget? Not only was Lucy

38

Smythe blonde and beautiful, head girl and captain of any sports activity in which the school fielded a team, but she'd also stolen Kate's first serious boyfriend, and then refused to give him back. Oh yes, Kate remembered Lucy Smythe. She'd seriously tarnished Kate's view of fidelity ever since.

"How is dear Lucy?" she forced herself to ask.

"Just married a city lawyer, and sailing around the world on some ship for her honeymoon."

"What a pity the *Titanic*'s already sunk."

"The *Titanic*? And there was I thinking you'd forgiven her. Anyway, as I was saying, Mrs Smythe said why didn't I come round and we could watch the DVD of her wedding. Four daughters and all married. And where was my one and only daughter? At someone else's wedding and still refusing to have one of her own."

Now her mother sounded like Mrs Bennet from *Pride and Prejudice*, and Kate had no intention of auditioning for the role of Elizabeth. No-one, absolutely no-one, should have to listen to this, especially not after what she'd been through.

"Mother. Listen to me very carefully, because I am not saying this again. Nothing happened yesterday." Kate paused to check the size of her nose with her hand. "I know what you want me to say," she continued, encouraged by its static properties. "That my knight, who was caught having it off with someone else while I was engaged to him – not a long engagement, mind, just twelve weeks – that this tarnished knight would realise the error of his ways, res- urrect his trusty steed from the knacker's yard and, scooping me up into his arms, would carry me off kicking and screaming into the sunset, but it didn't happen. I know you and Dad had this wonderful relationship – flowers on every anniversary, moonlit dinners, etc. – but this is the twenty-first century. Women are…well, we don't need a man to feel complete. And even if we did – which we don't – people just don't behave like that these days."

"Saul would." Helen paused. "If you'd let him."

"You don't know that. You've only seen what he wanted you to see."

"You think your mother's some romantic old fool, don't you? But I'm not. And I know what I know. You could have had everything, my girl, this time. Everything, and you let it get away."

The kettle boiled. Kate tipped a generous helping of coffee and water into her mug. They were now on familiar territory. She could even envisage the scene back in Cambridge. Helen would be sitting in her favourite armchair looking across at a large black-and-white photograph of her wedding to Kate's father, framed majestically in antique silver, and standing proud on a round and highly polished mahogany table.

She'd be studying the photo and wondering how two such sensible and loving people could produce a daughter who wouldn't know a good man if she fell over one. Oh yes, Kate had heard this speech one hundred times before, and she was in no mood to make that one hundred and one.

"Mum, I'm thinking of coming up next weekend. I'll ring you later in the week. Must go now, else my bath will overflow. Love you." And before Helen could respond, Kate put the phone down and muttered a quick prayer for forgiveness.

When would her mother learn? She and Saul were finished. Finito. No longer an item. In whatever language her mother chose, the end result was always the same. They were no longer a couple.

And that was the way it was going to stay.

So why then was there a text from an unknown number flashing up at her from her iPhone, pricking at her curiosity with its connotations? To read or not to read? To reply or ignore? Or banish forever with that simple little button marked *delete?*

When the buzzer rang at twelve thirty on the dot, Kate still wasn't sure she'd made the right decision.

Need to discuss matters. Lunch? the text had read.

Since there was only one reason why Saul could possibly want to see her, Kate had finally agreed to their meeting. He was going to apologise, she told herself. To offer her an explanation for his behaviour last night. And, being the man he was, he was going to do it face to face.

"Come on up," she instructed through the intercom. "It's on the first floor, number 3, but then you probably already know that, since you seem to know everything else."

Glancing up quickly at her pale reflection in the hall mirror, she pulled her red silk blouse down so that it hung elegantly over a pair of black trousers, and swept her dark hair back behind her ears. Taking a deep breath, she opened the door.

No matter how many times she saw him, her heart would always miss a beat whenever their eyes first met. And now there Saul was, standing in front of her, casually dressed in slightly faded jeans and a pale blue checked shirt, with sleeves rolled up, and his two top buttons undone to display just a hint of what lay beneath.

Kate wondered if she still had the same effect on him. Probably not. Why should she? He was thirty-seven, a millionaire businessman with the physique of James Bond and his own private jet. Whereas she was twenty-eight, had the physique of a pixie, a pair of dodgy lungs and an even dodgier mother. She knew they said that love was blind, but it would have to be deaf and dumb as well to cast the pair of them together.

"Are you ready?"

She could detect a note of impatience. "Almost. You'd better come in, I won't be a minute." Kate dived into the kitchen to check she'd turned everything off, leaving Saul to cast a critical eye around the rest of the flat.

Set in a leafy suburb of south-east London, Ivy House had started life as a Victorian mansion for a local banker and his numerous children. Now, 130 years later, it contained five apartments, each having been sympathetically restored by a builder who'd been so impressed with his own handiwork that he'd moved into the basement.

"How long have you been here?" he asked.

"Just over a year," she called out to him from the kitchen. "Lydia and I decided that since we spend all day at work together, it was time we stopped living together too. So she's moved in with her boyfriend and I came here. I've not finished decorating though," Kate added quickly in case he thought the green wallpaper in the hallway was her choice.

"I see you've bought one of Jeff Long's paintings."

Kate returned to find him standing in front of her cast iron fireplace in the sitting room. He was examining an oil painting full of glorious colour, depicting the artist's view of Dartmoor. "Do you approve?" she asked, wondering why it should matter to her if he did or not.

"I wouldn't have given him an exhibition last year if I didn't. Sold most of his paintings during the preview, which was quite impressive, even for me." He turned round, that old familiar grin creeping across his lips. "Surprised to find you can afford him."

"Business has been good recently," she began defensively, "and you always said paintings were a good investment, so long as you buy what you like. And I do like him…" She tailed off, groaning inwardly. What was the matter with her? Now she sounded more like a petulant child than a connoisseur of art. "Shall we go?" Suddenly she wanted him out of her flat, out of her own private sanctuary. There were no memories of him here, and that was exactly how she wanted it to remain.

"I've booked a table at the bistro round the corner," Saul said, holding the door open for her. "Have you been there before?"

Kate shook her head. Why did she feel so nervous? It was Saul who should be nervous. Saul who should be grovelling at her feet, showering her red toenails with apologies, or at least something resembling an explanation for last night. But as he bounded down the stairs to open the front door, there was no air of humility in any part of that suave physique. No air of humility at all.

Kate had passed Mario's, in the heart of East Dulwich, many times before, but never in her wildest dreams had she expected to come here with Saul. An enthusiastic waiter escorted them to a table near the window, and left them alone to study the menu. In one of the corners, a trio of cello, saxophone and piano burst forth across the converted old chapel with rhythm and blues, while Kate found herself staring at a piece of card, trying to concentrate on its contents.

"What do you want?" she heard Saul ask.

"I think I'll just have soup, and a glass of white wine, thank you. And you?"

Saul handed the menu back to the waiter. "A strong black coffee. Nothing else for me. Thanks."

Kate couldn't resist a guarded smile. "Hangover?"

"No. Lack of sleep."

She wanted to empathise with him, but decided against it. The last thing she wanted was for him to know they had anything in common. "How did you get my mobile number?" she asked, desperate to change the subject. "It wasn't on the website."

"Your mother. For some strange reason, which I'm sure defeats you, she seems to like me. When I phoned to check your home address, in case I decided to post the invite, rather than deliver it in person to the office, she sent me a note with all your vital statistics."

Kate felt herself begin to colour.

"Not those vital statistics," he added quickly. "I could have sent them back with a note saying *thanks, but no thanks*, but that would have hurt her. And, contrary to your opinion of me, I don't like hurting middle-aged ladies."

"That's not fair and you know it. I've never accused you of hurting middle-aged ladies, just young ones."

"Touché." To Kate's surprise, he gave her one of his laid-back grins. This was Saul at his most mellow. He really must have a hangover, she thought with amusement.

"So what is it you want to see me about?" She leant back in her chair and folded her arms. This was the bit she was going to enjoy, the reason why she'd agreed to the meeting, when he would squirm with embarrassment as he tried to justify the previous evening. The only problem was that he didn't look as though he was in a squirming mood.

"I have a business proposition for you," he said, thanking the waiter for his coffee.

Kate almost choked. "A what?"

"You heard, and before you start your usual protestations, you could at least hear me out. I'm off to Majorca in a week's time, to visit Alicia Gonzalez, one of Spain's most promising new artists. She won't come to me, so I've got to go to her. And I need an interpreter."

"An interpreter?" What was happening here? This was not an apology. No way could anyone class this as an apology. "Isn't there something else you want to say?"

Saul seemed to consider it for a minute. "No. I don't think so."

"I see." She didn't, but something told her her lack of vision was not high on his list of priorities. "And you want an interpreter?"

He nodded.

"In which case, I know just the person for you."

"I don't want one of your interpreters, I want you."

Kate put her soup spoon down before she dropped it. Now she knew she should have pressed delete. "Why?" she asked, trying to keep calm. "Why me?"

"Because you've come personally recommended."

"By whom? And don't you dare say my mother."

"No, by me. You used to work for me, or have you forgotten?"

Suddenly Kate had lost her appetite. "I'm not in the mood for one of our silly conversations," she warned him, aware that discussing a business proposition after only a few hours' sleep was not a good idea. Especially when it involved Saul.

"Personal recommendation. That's the best way to do business. One of my father's cardinal rules."

"But your father left his company – your company – in a mess."

"That was because he wasn't a very good judge of character." He gulped down the last of his coffee before adding quietly, "But I am."

Kate couldn't look at him. She kept her eyes firmly on the bowl of untouched soup, only too aware of the chemistry that last comment had created. "I can't spare the time. I'm needed in the office. I've got a massive project due in next week," she told the swirls of carrot, as though they might be interested, "but if you'll let me recommend—"

"If you can't spare the time, I'll take my business elsewhere. I'm sure London is full of translation agencies which would bend over backwards to include the major shareholder of Preston Aviation amongst their clients."

Kate glanced up at him. He was trying to attract the waiter's attention. He was also trying to blackmail her, to introduce that nasty pound sign into her thoughts. And, to her dismay, it was working, because she knew he was right. They *did* need the prestige that his name would bring. They also needed his money too, as only last week Lydia had announced that the latest translation memory software was going to cost considerably more than either of them were expecting.

"All right," she said, hating herself for succumbing so easily, and putting profit before principle. "I'll go. But only on my terms."

Now she had his full attention. "Assuming we're staying overnight, I want separate rooms on separate floors at the hotel."

"Are you sure you don't want separate hotels?"

"Only if you think that will be necessary," she countered, refusing to be goaded by the lazy sarcasm in his voice. "And another thing: I want to discuss yesterday."

"There's nothing to discuss," he stated tersely.

But Kate wasn't to be dissuaded. "This is, as you say, a business proposition. That's what it must be. Nothing else."

Saul took a deep breath. "If you're referring to my behaviour last night, then you can rest assured. That was, as you so rightly said at the time, an act of madness. I was, how shall I put it, completely captivated by your charms, having consumed one bottle of wine too many. You have my word that nothing like that will ever happen again."

"Why – have you joined the Salvation Army?"

His face told her exactly what he thought of that suggestion, and Kate had to refrain from bursting out laughing. "I don't somehow see me going round banging a cymbal or preaching the gospel for abstinence, do you? Now, do I assume that you're not going to drink any more of your soup?"

She nodded, pushing her soup bowl away from her, its contents hardly touched.

"It's no wonder you've lost so much weight, if that's how you treat your food."

"There's nothing wrong with my appetite. I was fine until a few minutes ago. And I won't starve just because I haven't eaten this, because I actually had breakfast this morning. Two pieces of toast and…" She broke off abruptly. "Why am I justifying my eating habits to you?"

"I've absolutely no idea. Unless, of course, I've touched a raw nerve? Now, if you'll excuse me." With that, he pushed the chair back, and went off in search of their waiter and the bill.

The walk back to Kate's flat was a silent affair, with Saul belatedly wondering whether he should enrol himself on a crash course on how to charm ex-fiancées. He thrust his hands deep into his trouser pockets. And lesson one would be to impress upon males with hangovers the importance of excluding personal comments relating to alcohol consumption and weight loss, especially when discussing possible business ventures.

"Saul?"

"Hm?"

Kate had stopped outside the portico of her building, and was looking up at him with a typically inquisitive expression in those large, green eyes. "Last night…at the wedding…was Maria…was it awful after I'd left?"

"You mean, did you ruin the party?"

"No, that's not what I said. After all, I didn't start it."

He chose to ignore that comment, and wondered if he should leave her to suffer in ignorance, just as he'd suffered when she'd left him standing, centre stage, with the entire wedding party making up the audience. But he didn't have the energy or clarity of thought.

"Our performance didn't stop the party, if that's what you mean. There was a stunned silence for a few seconds, a lot of embarrassed muttering, and then the music was turned up and life continued."

He didn't add that he'd then had to explain his behaviour to Patti. Nor that he'd arranged for her to be taken home after she'd informed him he was the lowest form of pond life, an amoeba, a comment which had surprised him as, up until then, he'd shared Kate's preconception of her intelligence.

He should never have asked Dave, a friend since university days, if he could borrow his girlfriend. It had not been one of his more inspired ideas.

"Borrow my girl? God, man, what for? You can get anyone you want. I've seen the way women look at you when we're out. What do you want to borrow Patti for?"

"She's an actress, isn't she? I want to hire her to play a part. Do you think she'll agree?"

"She'll agree to anything at the moment that pays well. But why? What about that woman, sister of Brian's? You remember? Made a beeline for you at his son's christening last month. Saw her looking at you. Couldn't stop fluttering her eyelashes at you."

"I don't want her. I don't want anyone. It wouldn't be fair. To lead them on and then... I'm just not interested."

"You've got it bad again, haven't you? Thought you'd got over it."

Saul felt that all too familiar pang of emptiness twist deep within his stomach. Until he'd heard Kate's dulcet tones ring out across the office, telling him she'd rather burn in hell than talk to him, so had he.

"Do you want me to give you a price? I can work one out for you tomorrow."

"What?"

Kate's voice jolted him back to the present. "For the interpreting?

I'm afraid I don't come cheap, and I would expect you to pay all expenses: travel, hotel costs, etc."

"I trust you, but if it makes you feel any better, send me an email." Pulling out his wallet, Saul removed a business card and handed it to her. "Just in case you've forgotten."

And for a second, their fingers touched.

"Kate…"

"Yes?"

He cleared his throat, but he couldn't continue. He couldn't tell her what he knew she wanted him to say: that this afternoon was just a figment of her imagination.

"I'm going away tomorrow," he said, pulling his key fob from out of his pocket, "first thing, for a few days, but I'll phone you when I'm back to let you know the details. And in the meantime, do you think you could do something for me?"

"Something else, you mean?"

The corners of his lips twitched. "Could you try and stop worrying, as though you've got a date with Dracula? This is business, Kate, pure and simple, as you yourself said, not a trip to bloody Transylvania!"

Chapter 5

Men! Kate could do without them. Especially ex-fiancés, and those who drove their Land Rovers through Wimbledon as though they were rehearsing for the Dakar Rally. She glanced down at her stockings. A few minutes ago, they'd resembled the pale, blemish-free legs on the packaging. Now, thanks to some moron and an enormous pool of water, they wouldn't have looked out of place on a hippopotamus.

Thank God she'd got a spare pair in the office. She'd change into them as soon as she arrived and then work out a quote for Saul. Strange how some things never change. Three years on and once again she was helping him to converse with his fellow Europeans.

When Kate had first been hired, Saul had still been managing director of Preston Aviation, rather than just having a seat on the board. He'd been in the middle of negotiating the purchase of an Airbus A320 from a company in Frankfurt and had asked his secretary to find him a good technical German translator. Someone who was not only fluent in the language, but would be willing to accompany him to Germany when he flew out later that month.

Kate was then a freelance translator with a global translation company. She'd just returned from her first major interpreting assignment, when the agency had phoned her in a panic. The man they'd hired was ill. Could she help?

Her knowledge of aircraft had been instrumental; a knowledge gained from years of listening to her father. "Can you hear that, Kate?" he would say. "That growl has to be a Griffin engine." Or, "You can tell a Victor by the crescent shape of its wing." He'd worked as an engineer for an aircraft conversion company near Cambridge, living and breathing his passion for the miracle of flight, and Kate had loved her father, following him from air show to air show, lapping up every story he could relate.

It was the one thing she had over the Lucy Smythes of this world. She certainly knew her elevators from her ailerons!

"Did you have a good weekend?" Tim asked, as Kate squelched her way across the office.

She attempted an enthusiastic nod, but it petered out halfway through. "It's complicated," she said, realising that that was probably the understatement of the century. "Did you need me for anything?"

"Will tell you later, once you've had your morning fix of coffee."

Not even caffeine, though, nor a dry pair of stockings, could spur Kate into action that particular morning. She couldn't concentrate. And she needed to concentrate if she was going to meet all the deadlines that week. Her mind, though, was elsewhere, doodling its way around her notepad, as she berated herself over and over again for agreeing to accompany Saul.

What had she thought she was doing – going to Majorca with

her ex? A man who, until recently, had been neatly tucked away, where he belonged, in the dim and distant past? Who, even now, only wanted her for business?

A contract between two professional people, he'd said. So why couldn't she look at it like that? Why couldn't she focus on the fundamentals? That she was no longer some pathetic fool with aspirations of romance, but an independent woman of the twenty-first century, who only needed men for sex.

Sex? Kate stopped and looked down at her doodlings, which were becoming more and more intense. Oh God, it had been good. No, better than that. Sex had been wonderful, and no amount of careful propaganda could convince her otherwise. The magnificence of that body, that powerful physique which exuded virility with every move it made. Which would tempt and tease, with tantalising promises of things to come, as they glided across the sheets, merging and moving in an erotic rhythm all of their own. The exhilarating ecstasy of his kisses setting her soul alight, as he drew her closer and closer until...

Kate sighed, stopped and crossed her legs tightly together. Very tightly indeed. Yes, it was probably just as well it was going to be a business arrangement. Anything else was just asking for trouble!

From across the room, a printer sprang to life. Must be Tim printing out a job, she thought, absentmindedly. But instead of wandering over to see what it was, Kate made her way towards the wastepaper basket.

There really was only one thing to do, she decided, crumpling up her doodlings and binning them. She needed to visit the art gallery. To see if she could lay old ghosts to rest, and she had to do it now, today, while she knew he was going to be away, as then and only then could she begin to move forward.

Perhaps she should have done it years ago. Yet, until this weekend, she hadn't been aware of the need. She'd thought she was over him. Well and truly over him.

Tim looked up as Kate put her head around the door. "I'm having an early lunch," she said, hoping he wouldn't ask why.

"No problem." He paused and stroked the stubble on one of his double chins thoughtfully. "You know, if there's anything I can help you with... I know you usually confide in Lydia, and she's away this week, but if you want to discuss anything, I'm an excellent listener, for what it's worth."

There were times when Kate had to resist the overpowering urge to go and hug him for being so nice. The genial expression on that chubby face made Kate wish she was attracted to him, that Tim really was the boyfriend Saul imagined him to be.

"Thanks for the offer, but I think I can manage this one on my own." Then, remembering his presence earlier this morning, she added, "Did you want to see me for something?"

"This Friday – are you doing anything?"

Kate shook her head. "I'm going to Cambridge to see Mum on Saturday but nothing on Friday. Why?"

"I've got tickets for *Phantom*. Want to come?" The pleasure that radiated across Kate's face answered his question. "Good. We'll have dinner first. Don't worry, leave it all to me."

And Kate did, grateful for the support. Now, though, she had to go and exorcise a phantom of her own.

*

It had been a beautiful spring morning, three years ago, when Kate first arrived at the impressive headquarters of Preston Aviation. Situated in the heart of the city, cascading lifts of glass and gleaming marble floors moulded into seamless walls, upon which hung as varied a collection of modern art as she'd ever seen.

As usual, she was early. Could she wait? Yes, there, by a pair of imposing oak doors. Mr Preston would see her as soon as he was ready. He'd been working late last night, his secretary, a tall, grey-haired lady in a no-nonsense pinstriped trouser suit, told her. He wouldn't keep her waiting long. Did she want a coffee?

Before Kate could say "yes", a voice boomed through the intercom. "Show Mr Walters in."

Her heart missed a beat. "Didn't the agency phone?"

The elderly woman opposite nodded, and seemed surprised. "I sent him an email before I left last Friday. It's not like him not to read his post. Never mind, just knock on the door, and go in. And," she remarked as an afterthought, "don't let him bully you."

The tale of Jack and the Beanstalk whirled through Kate's mind. And at that precise moment, she wasn't sure she was in the mood for an encounter with a bad-tempered giant.

"His bark really is worse than his bite," his secretary added encouragingly.

Kate wanted to ask how she assessed the size of his bite, but decided against it. After all, she wasn't a coward. She could handle whatever lay on the other side. She could...

"Who are you?"

...spend all day looking at the most attractive man she'd ever seen. The only problem was that he didn't seem too pleased to see her.

"Well, do you have a voice?"

"Of course. I'm… I'm…"

"Yes?"

"Kate Fenton." That was it. "I'm the interpreter." She offered her hand.

"Oh, no, you're not," he said, taking it and refusing to give it back. "You're certainly not the interpreter, not unless our Mr Walters is a cross-dresser."

Daring to glance up, she thought she saw a trace of amusement crease the fine lines of disapproval. But only for a second. His features were now as aggressively dismissive as when she had first entered. If he could have pressed a button to have her ejected, she knew he'd have used it.

"I take it Mr Walters couldn't come, then," he said, finally releasing her. "I see. So they sent me you. You'd better sit down." He didn't appear to be too impressed with the situation.

Neither, though, was Kate. "I'll stand, thank you." She waited until he'd repositioned himself on the swivel chair behind his desk. Now she had height on her side. "Mr Walters has flu. And I understand from your secretary that you were informed. That she sent you an email last Friday before she left." She paused, noticing one eyebrow being raised disbelievingly. "Perhaps you didn't open it?"

"Do I look like a man who doesn't open his emails?" He leant back in his chair and linked his hands together, as though he were sizing up the weight of his opponent.

"No, but…but we all make mistakes…"

"You might make mistakes, Ms Fenton. The agency has certainly made a mistake. I can't afford to make mistakes."

"Well, lucky you." It was out before Kate could stop herself, and stealing a glance at her antagonist, she wondered if he'd lost the eject button all together.

"You think I'm lucky, do you? You'll forgive me if I don't view this situation in quite the same light. Someone, somewhere, has made a mistake and I've been sent you. The question is, what are we going to do about it?"

"I am not a mistake," she informed him indignantly. "I come to you highly recommended. I may not be as old as Mr Walters, who by the way is not *that* old, but I'm extremely well qualified in this area."

His face told her that he didn't believe this. A face that Kate would have classed as beautifully sculpted, if only he would allow some of those features to relax occasionally.

"I'm fluent in French, German, Spanish and Italian," she continued, trying to ignore what those features were doing to her. "My mother's mother was French, but she lived in Switzerland, which was where I spent most of my summer holidays. I studied German at university, with Spanish as my second language, for which I got a first. And before I went freelance, I spent over a year in Germany, working for a number of different companies."

"You misunderstand me," Saul said, pulling himself up from his chair, his voice coiling around her. "I'm not questioning your linguistic skills, just your technical ones. Aircraft to women are those things you have to go on when you want to sun yourself in one of the world's hotspots. You get on them, moan about the food, and then delight in selecting some foul-smelling perfume, before finally disembarking with never a thought for the poor sods who have transported you there. What can you possibly know about, for example, the range of an aircraft?"

Now Kate was bristling. "That was possibly the most chauvinistic load of rubbish I have ever heard."

"Chauvinistic, maybe, but not rubbish. I've yet to meet a woman who knows the difference between a Boeing 737-400 and a Boeing 737-800."

"The 800 has a taller fin than the 400." Aha! Now she had him. She could feel a sudden shift in the balance of power. All she had to do was go in for the kill. "You're interested in buying an A320 which, as anyone with any knowledge would tell you, was the world's first short-haul fly-by-wire airliner."

His eyes narrowed. "You have been doing your homework. Where did you get all this information from?"

"Oh, it was nothing. You know what we girls are like. I was having my nails done one evening, and struck up the most amazing conversation with my manicurist."

For a moment, he looked confused. Then, with a laugh, so richly self-deprecating that it sent most of Kate's preconceptions scurrying for shelter, he acknowledged her sarcasm.

"Very good," he said, moving around to the front of his desk to take a closer look at her. "No doubt I deserved that, but I'm impressed. No, I'm serious. Bad-tempered I may be, especially when I've not yet had breakfast, but I'm not totally beyond redemption. Although, I can tell by your expression that you're not sure whether you agree. Can I get you something? Or shall we just start again?"

"A coffee would be nice," Kate hazarded tentatively, sinking as gracefully as she could into the chair directly behind her. She'd just glimpsed a layer of charm beneath the aggression, and she wasn't sure which she found more disturbing.

"June, two coffees, please," he instructed through the intercom, perching on the corner of his desk, his legs, those long, suit-clad, muscular legs, just inches away from her fingers. "How do you like it?"

"Sorry?"

"Your coffee?"

"Oh, white, please, no sugar."

"Did you hear that, June? And could you bring in the Frankfurt A320 file, please? Ms Fenton will be joining us for a couple of weeks."

"I will? The agency has only booked me for a week," Kate ventured, wondering whether this act of boldness would cause his newly discovered humanity to vanish.

"I'll phone them up and tell them the business might take longer than first anticipated. After all, I'm buying an aircraft, not a book from Amazon. What are you smiling at?"

"Only that five minutes ago you couldn't wait to see the last of me, and now you're extending my contract, without me having translated a single word. I was just thinking that I might add unpredictable to my list of your qualities."

"Along with chauvinist? Did your research not inform you that I'm a difficult sod? Surely the tabloid press must have thrown up some intriguing, and probably totally fictitious, comments on my past?

"I don't read tabloids," Kate retorted. "And I wasn't studying you as a man, just your company."

"Thanks." Saul directed this last comment at his secretary, who had entered carrying a tray with one cup and one mug of coffee, together with two croissants, and a file tucked under her arm. He sprang up to relieve her of the load.

"The bakery apologised for being so late to deliver, Saul, but they're short-staffed, or something."

"You can tell them that Ms Fenton has them to thank for me almost biting her head off this morning." He passed Kate her cup of coffee. "Breakfast is an essential way to start the day, and it was late. Perhaps you could also tell them that, if it happens again, I might think about giving that new patisserie down the road a try. That should hopefully ensure I'm fed at the right time. Right, Ms Fenton..." He pulled out some sheets of A4 paper from the front of the file and handed them to her. "Or may I call you...what was it? Kate?"

She nodded obligingly, taking the sheets from him.

"I've got a meeting in ten minutes, which should last an hour. When I come back, I need to know what they say. Any problems, we can discuss them then. But first, if you'll excuse me, I'm going to have my breakfast."

With that Saul picked up the tray, and strode towards his private quarters at the opposite end of the room.

Kate leant back in the chair, clutching her cup. She'd met the giant and survived. And they could chop down that beanstalk whenever they liked, because she was perfectly happy where she was.

Chapter 6

It was beginning to rain again by the time Kate reached the gallery. The journey to Grenville Fine Arts had taken her slightly longer than she'd expected, but then she'd never had to make the trip from Wimbledon before. The last time she was here, standing outside a beautifully restored Georgian building off Piccadilly, she'd travelled in from St Paul's, where she'd been working.

The weather had been different back then, too. The city was in the midst of a late August heatwave. The air was sultry, full of the fumes from the day. And Kate could feel the constriction, lurking in her lungs, long before she'd arrived at her destination: one of London's prestigious venues for modern art.

"Don't start without me," she'd begged Saul over breakfast. "I may be a little late tonight but I want to help. I want to know everything there is to know about cataloguing for an exhibition."

And he'd smiled, that long, lascivious smile, and promised he'd wait; that when they walked down the aisle in just under a month's time, they would be partners in every sense of the word. Just the thought of his words, of the commitment in his voice, caused a warm feeling to flow through her veins, which

Kate knew had nothing to do with the heat outside.

Opening the door to his gallery, she had crossed over the threshold. Behind her was the chaos of a sultry summer's evening. Inside, there was silence, punctuated by a crescendo of voices coming from one of the rooms to the back of the building.

"Saul?" she queried as she walked across the floor towards them. "I know I'm a little early, but I thought we could…" The words died on her lips as Saul's assistant, a dark-haired beauty with the figure of Aphrodite, appeared before her. Only Claudia wasn't rushing across the room to greet Kate, like some Greek goddess. She was trying to get past her, to reach the main door. Her brilliant blue eyes fixing Kate's with a frenzy Kate wasn't expecting, a dislike that burnt through any pretence of friendship. But before Kate could utter a greeting, a farewell, or any other form of speech, Claudia flung open the door and, with a shriek bordering on the hysterical, fled out into the night.

Kate could only stand and stare. Her imagination was in free fall as snapshots of the young woman's appearance raced through her mind like a slideshow on speed. Her dress ripped away at the front. Her breasts exposed. Her perfume, so thick and pungent, so overpowering that it smothered any rational thought, until nothing was left. Nothing, that was, except the obvious. The only scenario that made any sense.

Turning round, she found Saul standing behind her, watching her. The already concerned expression on his face changed to total disbelief when he caught sight of the expression on Kate's.

She could remember that. She could remember it all so clearly. The moment when her whole world disintegrated around her.

When memories of the previous week came flooding back to taunt her. How Lady Horsham had flung herself at Saul at some charity do. How he'd reassured Kate that it was nothing, that he was just being polite to a patron of the arts and a benefactor of the poor. And how, gullible idiot that she was, she'd believed him.

Now, though, as he stood before her, as Kate hurriedly checked the buttons on his shirt, the zip on his trousers, his face for signs of lipstick, his whole physique for any signs of arousal, she was no longer sure. The fact that she couldn't find any didn't mean anything. Perhaps she'd interrupted them in the early stages of their affair, before Claudia could dangle her obvious assets in front of him, or plant those large red lips all over her beloved's face, and cause those hormones to come crashing through? Those same hormones which had found her, Kate, so desirable less than twenty-four hours earlier, when he'd made love to her?

How could he – how could he do this to her! After everything she'd told him about her issues with trust? About Lucy and the prom dance, and that guy at uni, with his promises of love? Did Saul not realise she didn't have the strength to go through it all again – to stand back and watch while he broke her heart?

For a few interminable seconds, it was all Kate could do to breathe, let alone speak. Then, as though she were on a film set and someone had just shouted "action", she tore off her engagement ring, a work of art, with emeralds encrusted in a white gold design, and flung it across the floor. The sound split the air between them with such force, until it finally landed at his feet.

"Kate, you've got it all wrong…"

"I don't think so." And with that, she turned her back on

him, and through sheer willpower propelled her legs across the threshold of his gallery for the very last time.

Behind her there was silence. He didn't say another word. He didn't make any attempt to restrain her. And Kate thought her heart would break, as she closed the door behind her; that her legs would buckle and refuse to support the weight of so much despair. It was over. There was no such thing as romance. Never again would she let her guard down. Never again would she allow anyone access to her love; it would be banished to the deepest recesses of her heart.

And first thing tomorrow morning, all their material goods would suffer the same fate. Anything Saul had bought her, and that was nearly everything, would be returned to him. She would hire a courier. It didn't matter how much it cost her, but by the time she'd finished, it would be over. There'd be no trace he'd ever existed.

"Can I help?" an enthusiastic voice broke through her thoughts. "Would you like a catalogue? The exhibition is open until the end of July, and features four of our most exciting new artists..."

Nothing had changed, and yet everything was different. Kate was confused, so confused, and no matter how hard she tried to rationalise her feelings, and put them back into some sort of order, she couldn't.

Time might have moved on, but she hadn't. The pain, lies and tears were all still there, lurking just beneath the surface, as fresh today as they were back then, when Saul had finally gathered his wits about him, and followed her out into the night.

*

Kate didn't hear him at first. The roar of the traffic from the main street, of Londoners revelling in the pubs and clubs, blotted out any thoughts but those whirling around in her imagination. It was only when she heard him call her name, a voice so compelling in its urgency, that she stopped and turned to face him.

"This is not what you think," Saul said, as she tried to catch her breath. "You've got to give me a chance to explain."

"Explain?" Kate gasped, looking back up at him, at the anxiety in his face, in his eyes, in every part of that suave physique, but it was too late. Her chest was tightening, the humidity of the night, the shock, his presence all bearing down on her with such a force that it was all she could do to breathe, let alone speak. "I don't…" she began, but she couldn't continue.

"Your inhaler," he groaned in desperation. "You need your inhaler. Where the hell is it?" he asked, grabbing her bag from her.

"I don't know." Kate wanted to cry out, to scream at him, but she couldn't. That would have involved energy, and she didn't have any. Instead, she slid down gracefully on to the pavement, the heat seeping through her cool cotton dress, and watched, helpless, as Saul rummaged through her bag and retrieved the little blue piece of plastic. Crouching down beside her, he pushed the device into her hand.

"Take it, Kate," he begged. "Please, take it."

Kate didn't need to be asked twice. She did as instructed, continuously, but it wasn't working. Both of them could see it wasn't working.

"I'm phoning for an ambulance," he said, as she struggled to exhale. "I'm phoning for one right now."

Kate tried to shake her head, to tell him she'd be fine, if only he'd go away and leave her to choke in peace, but both of them knew that wasn't true. And so she watched in desperation as he pulled out his mobile, and wondered if this was it. If she was really destined to die a breathless wreck in front of the only man she'd ever really loved, who even now was trying his damndest to save her from herself – and from a life without him.

Kate bit her bottom lip and glanced up. She was back in the gallery. The ghosts were slowly receding, slipping back into the past where they belonged. And in their place, a new assistant was peering up at her intently, from behind a pair of designer glasses.

"Do I know you?" the girl asked. "I'm sure we've met."

"I don't think so," Kate said quickly, hoping fervently that they hadn't, as the last thing she needed right now was to be recognised.

Turning her back on the elfin face, she grabbed a catalogue and wandered through to the exhibition room, to the first of the four artists. Liam O'Connor. A man after her own heart, who'd caused quite a stir recently by removing all his paintings from a national exhibition, due to the inclusion of an artist who'd slept with his wife.

His landscapes were bold and brazen. Each layer splashed thick with oil, worked and reworked until, finally, he was pleased with what he saw. A multitude of colours, a frenzy of passion which Kate would have bought on sight, if only she'd had the wall space, or bank balance to match.

Turning her attention to the other, less well-known artists, she drifted towards an exaggerated splash of colour entitled *Cornish Sunrise*.

"I like this artist's work," she said, aware she was still being watched. "I love the colours she uses…"

"I thought you would."

The hairs on her back shot up. But Saul was away. For a few days, he'd said, else she'd never have come.

"What are you doing here?" she burst out, before she could stop herself.

"The meeting was cancelled at the last minute. I arrived at the airport, only to get a text to say that the owner was ill, and could we reschedule?"

"Was… Was it important?"

"No, not really. I'm trying to buy a property up north, and this one came up for sale, so I thought I would go and have a look at it and see to some other matters while I was up there." He stopped and regarded her critically. "That explains my whereabouts this morning. Now I'd like to hear about yours."

"My what?"

"Whereabouts. What are you doing here?"

"Doing here?" Kate repeated blankly.

"Yes. Here in the gallery?" Then, as though he'd suddenly become aware they weren't alone, he turned to the woman in the glasses. "Mandy, how about taking your lunch hour now? I'm back for the rest of the day, so you don't need to worry about rushing back."

"I'm quite happy to stay."

"I'm sure you are. But I've got some post for you to get out later, so now would be an excellent time for you to satisfy that amazing appetite of yours. It will also give me an opportunity to work out what I want to say."

"OK," she acquiesced. "If you're sure? Oh, and by the way, your sister phoned to find out how you were. I thought she was supposed to be on her honeymoon?"

Saul ignored the unvoiced question. "Anything else?"

"Yes, the estate agents phoned. Wanted to know if you'd thought—"

"I'll deal with that later," he cut in quickly. "On second thoughts, where are you going for your lunch?"

"I can go in any direction you want me to."

"Could you go into their offices round the corner, and either try and see Keith Drew or leave a message for him? Could you tell him that he's not to do anything without talking to me first?"

Mandy gave him such an obliging smile Kate wished she could have sight of her job specification.

"Right," Saul said once Mandy had left. "Now we've got some privacy."

"I don't need privacy. As it so happens, I was on my way out too."

She made to move past him, but Saul stood his ground. "You're not going anywhere until you've answered one or two of my questions. You see, while I was driving back from the airport, wondering what other disasters today had in store for me, the last thing I expected to do was to walk into my gallery and see you standing there. And now I'm wondering why. Why, after all these years, you've decided to pay me a visit." He stopped, his voice suddenly hardening. "It wasn't me, though, that you decided to visit, was it? You thought I was going to be away. So why have you come here?"

Get out of this one, Kate thought to herself ruefully. "Do I need a reason to visit an art gallery?"

"Yes. Yes, you do, when it's mine. Shall I tell you what I think went round your mind this morning?"

"I really don't think this is necessary..."

"Oh, but I do. You see, I think you woke up this morning and thought, he cheated on me once before. I don't know if I can trust him. If I go round to his gallery while he's away, I can check up on him. Check that there is a painter called Alicia Gonzalez, and that he's meant to be visiting her next week."

Kate felt the ground beneath her feet begin to crumble. What was he talking about? She opened her mouth to protest her innocence, to this crime at least, but the words wouldn't come.

"I see by your silence I'm right." He gave a harsh laugh. "Trust. Such a small word, so difficult to do." He strode across towards the desk. Taking off his suit jacket, still glistening with the morning's weather, he threw it across the back of the chair.

Kate couldn't tear her eyes away from him, from the sight of that white shirt, now exposed and slightly damp in places from the rain, clinging tenaciously to his chest. It provided what she already knew, that he had one hell of a body.

Unfortunately, he also had a habit of turning up when he wasn't wanted. How could she prepare herself for their forthcoming trip, if he kept reappearing and cross-examining her as though he were counsel for the prosecution?

"Why would I lie to you? What could I possibly gain?" Saul paused as a flash of understanding streaked across his face. "Unless, of course, you still flatter yourself that I might be interested in you? Am I on the right track? You thought to yourself, after the other night, when you left me standing in the middle of the dance floor, that I might still be attracted to you. That I might have devised a plan to whisk you away to some godforsaken country, maroon you in some hotel, or even worse, some cottage in the middle of nowhere, and make love to you – mad, passionate love."

The savage way in which he flung those words at her filled Kate with dismay. He couldn't have been further from the truth if he'd tried, but the anger, the pure, naked anger, had stripped her of any response.

What could she say? That she'd only come here today to test herself? To see if she was over him? How could she tell him that?

"What – has the cat got your tongue? That's not like you. At least it's not like the you I used to know, but then you've become very successful since you threw my love back at me, haven't you? You and Lydia. Well, I'm glad our time together wasn't a total waste."

"If you're implying…" At last Kate had found her voice. She also realised her chest was beginning to tighten. Time, once again, was not on her side.

"I'm not implying anything," he retorted. "I'm delighted to know you've done so well, that you managed to start a small business and turn it into one with a turnover of half a million pounds in less than two years."

"Have you been keeping tabs on me?"

"No, just keeping an eye on a protégée. Just following her first steps on the ladder to fame and fortune. Trouble is, my dear, it doesn't bring happiness. It doesn't keep you warm at night."

"Not like Patti." Thank God she'd remembered her name.

"Patti?" For a moment, he appeared genuinely surprised. Then, "Oh, her."

Did he have that many, that he couldn't remember their names? What had happened to him during the last few years? This wasn't the Saul she'd known and loved. Certainly not the Saul of her memories.

Afraid that any second her lungs would burst, or her heart would break for the man she'd adored, Kate knew she had to leave, to get out of the building before she broke down completely. She'd been a fool to come here today. A fool to think she could re-examine her past with the impartiality of a historian. She couldn't. It was still too recent, too alive. And, as she finally closed the door behind her and fumbled for her puffer, she had a horrible feeling it always would be.

Saul slumped down at his desk and groaned. He sank his head into his hands and pressed his palms hard against his temples. He didn't know what else to do.

The trip to Majorca was genuine. He needed an interpreter. He also needed Kate. He needed to spend some time alone with her, to try and make her see that he was still the same man with whom she'd fallen in love. It was an attempt to combine business with pleasure, to remind her how well they worked together and leave the chemistry between them to do the rest.

He knew it was still there. He'd felt it on Saturday, as he'd held her in his arms, and she hadn't resisted. Not at first, that was. She'd even allowed him to kiss her, not a half-hearted gesture from an ex-lover, but a groin-pulsating embrace from someone who wanted more, so much more. And she'd responded, giving him cause to hope.

The door opened and his head shot up, but it wasn't Kate, the woman he wanted to see. It wasn't even Mandy. It was the postman, reminding him that time was short, that he needed to get a grip on things and compose himself.

Pulling himself up out of the chair, Saul wandered through to the cloakroom at the end of the gallery and ran some cold water into the basin. He splashed it over his face, and straightening up, looked at his reflection in the ebony-edged mirror. The lines appeared more furrowed, and the mouth more set in its way.

He wanted to settle down, to have children. He'd worked hard all his life, ever since he could remember, and now he wanted to enjoy the fruits of all his labour. But he didn't want to settle down with just anyone. He wanted Kate. The only problem was that she still didn't want him. And, after the way he'd behaved this afternoon, who could blame her? He wouldn't blame her if she never spoke to him again.

Chapter 7

Tim stood in the doorway to Kate's office. "Are you ready?" he asked. "Only we should leave now, if we want to eat before the show."

"I've just finished." Kate closed the file on the computer screen. "I'm so sorry, I didn't realise it was so late."

"You never do. One of these days, you'll fall asleep at this thing, and the next morning, instead of finding a Kate Fenton, we'll find an additional computer!"

"Oh, I do hope not. You'd look a bit silly taking a computer out to the theatre." She slipped her arms through the jacket he was holding open for her. "But you might have a point. It's just that this week has been so busy, and if I'm supposed to be going to Majorca on Monday, I just wanted to—"

"I know. Make sure everything is up to date, and that we all have enough instructions, including the clause on what to do if we're suddenly invaded by little green men." Tim gave her an affectionate pat on the shoulder. "I don't know about you, but I'm in need of sustenance. Let's worry about the Martians later, shall we, and go and eat."

*

The restaurant he'd chosen was located down one of the numerous side streets near to the theatre. There were no signs advertising its existence. No boards inviting the hungry theatregoer to sample its cuisine. Nothing, in fact, to declare its presence on this planet as anything other than a private residence.

Yet when Tim swung open the doors, Kate felt as though she'd entered a parallel universe. A universe in which olive-skinned waiters swirled round from table to table, squeezing between the hordes of diners, their animated voices bellowing out against the clattering and crashing of plates from the kitchen. All she needed now was for the swing doors on the other side of the room to burst open and Marlon Brando to appear.

"Are you sure you're not related to the Mafia?" she asked as a 'second cousin once removed' led them to a small table, sporting a wine-stained checked tablecloth and an impressive array of breadsticks.

"Nope." Tim grinned and passed her the menu.

"Or come from another planet? It's just that every time we go out, you always manage to find some place I've never ever heard of, and that, if I tried to find it again, would have disappeared in a puff of smoke. It's like being in one of those films. You know, the ones where if I went out of that door now, and tried to come back in, I'd probably find myself in some elderly lady's sitting room, and no-one would believe my story, so I'd be carried off to some far away institution, where I'd stay until someone from the future travelled back in time to rescue me, and save the world from destruction by robots!"

Tim leant back in his seat, struggling to open a defiant pack of breadsticks. "You're amazing, do you know that?"

"I am?"

"Yep. And whatever happens during the next few days, you just remember that. That your Uncle Timothy thinks you're one truly amazing woman. Now," he continued, as the waiter appeared to take their orders, "what would you like?"

What Kate would really have liked was to fast-forward to next weekend. She knew she was being disloyal to Tim and to her mother, but she couldn't help it. She didn't want to go to Majorca with Saul, and at this moment, she would do anything to get out of it.

"Kate, what do you want?"

"Sorry? Oh, Tim, forgive me. I'll have...um...the lasagne, please, and could I have a small jug of water?"

"No wine?"

Kate shook her head. "Please don't let me stop you. I just need a clear head..."

"For tomorrow?" Tim finished her sentence and shook his head sadly.

"I'm sorry. I'm ruining our evening. Forgive me?" She struggled to give him a reassuring smile, which, to her surprise, actually worked. Now all she had to do was keep the conversation superficial, the mood light, and he would regard their evening as an overwhelming success.

And she could do this. She really could. She could put Saul out of her mind, at least for tonight. After all, it wasn't the first time she'd had to banish him from her thoughts. She'd spent the last few years telling herself he didn't exist, that their love had been a diversion – albeit, at times, a very pleasant diversion – but that was all. And whenever she'd begun to falter, and the longing had begun to resurface, she'd conjured up that night in the gallery, and congratulated herself on a lucky escape.

Now, though, she couldn't do that. She had a new scenario to consider. A scenario in which the principal actor had hurled abuse at her and accused *her* of not trusting *him!* Kate took a sip of her water. And what had he done, when he'd calmed down? Instead of sending her an apology, or filling the office with flowers, which she'd have binned immediately, he'd sent her an email with their travel itinerary, and a slightly worrying postscript.

Since I understand you're staying with your mother (was nothing private these days?) *and my plane is based near Cambridge, I'm proposing to spend the weekend at the Manor.* Kate broke off. So he still had the house which was to have been their home. Why? Why hadn't he sold it? And why did she have a horrible feeling she knew what was coming next?

In an attempt to help the government in their quest for a greener planet, I suggest you leave your petrol-guzzling deathtrap of a vehicle behind and allow me the pleasure of giving you a lift. And then, as though he knew exactly what she would say, *If you're thinking of protesting, and can't stand the thought of spending an additional couple of hours in my company, just view it as working overtime and bill it to the gallery.*

Kate picked up her pen. "Right," she said, fuming at the arrogance of the man. "If he insists on interfering in my private life and insulting my clapped-out old Mini, then he can jolly well pay for the privilege." Next to the newly printed itinerary, she scribbled,

NB: additional charge for antisocial hours. Depending upon antisocial nature of client, possible surcharge upon that. To be decided.

"What do you think?"

Tim was looking at her expectantly as though he was waiting for an answer. The only problem was that Kate was totally unaware of the question. The words 'witches' and 'Jack Nicholson' came to mind, but unfortunately, that was about it. "Could you say that again?" she wanted to ask, but she didn't dare. It was just too rude to sit opposite a friend, a surrogate boyfriend, no less, and not listen to a word he'd said. So Kate played with what she could recall.

"Jack Nicholson?" she said, trailing her fork along the remains of the sauce on her plate, when she could prevaricate no longer. "Brilliant actor. I think he was excellent in *The Witches of Eastwick*."

She sought his face anxiously for some sign of success, to know she'd gambled successfully. She didn't have to wait long, though, to know she'd failed miserably. Tim threw his head back and let out such a roar of laughter that the waiter passing almost jumped out of his waistcoat and sent a tray of drinks spinning into orbit.

"I was talking about Roald Dahl," he informed her, once he'd caught his breath. "I need some ideas for my nephew."

Still Kate looked puzzled.

"I think you misunderstood my 'have you seen *The Witches*, you know, the film with Anjelica Huston, who used to have a relationship with Jack Nicholson?' for something else. No, don't look so guilty. What are we going to do with you, Kate?"

"Shoot me?" At least then she wouldn't have to travel up to

Cambridge with her own personal wizard. "But could you do it after the show?"

It was only later, when Kate was truly immersed in the passionate spectacle being performed in front of her, that Saul's image once more cast its shadow across her heart. Only then did she allow herself to remember, to feel the touch of those lips, to see the hunger in those dark eyes as he'd drawn her towards him.

Only then did she allow herself a glimpse of the truth: that despite everything he could throw at her, he still moved her. That all she really wanted to do was rush out of the theatre and scan the streets of London until she found him, with an orchestra playing in the background, and a breeze billowing through her hair. And then…

And then, there he would be, lounging indolently against some bar, with a blonde – it had to be a blonde – on one or both arms. He would catch sight of her in a mirror and smile, that sensual smile of unsurpassed pleasure, and then…

And then, the dream would start to fade, and the nightmare begin.

She pulled out another sweet from Tim's proffered bag. This was positively the last time she'd allow herself time off to go and watch a love story. She must need her brain examined. She was not the heroine on stage, being fêted by two men. To her knowledge, she wasn't even being fêted by one man.

She was, or at least had been until a week ago, Kate Fenton, successful businesswoman, with no personal complications. And that, if she were to keep her sanity, was the way it had to stay.

"Is that all you're taking?" Saul asked, surveying the numerous bags outside Kate's front door the following morning. "Are you quite sure there's nothing you've forgotten?"

Kate cast an anxious eye over her belongings. "No, I don't think so." Then, as Saul disappeared back down the stairs with her luggage, Kate darted back into the flat. "I won't be a minute," she called out to him over her shoulder.

She knew she'd forget something; she always did. And there, leaning to one side in the kitchen sink, was a large bunch of sweet-smelling stocks. Whisking them out of the basin, she quickly wrapped them up in their original paper, then ran back down the stairs, almost colliding with Saul, who was on his way up to find her.

"I didn't know you cared," he remarked wryly, when he saw what she was clutching. "But since you've gone to all this effort, I accept."

"They're not for you, they're for..." But their destination died on her lips. Why was he looking at her like that, with that decidedly provocative glint in those dark eyes? This journey was supposed to be about pooling resources and saving the world, not a trip down memory lane. "Excuse me, please, but you're in my way."

"And you – or to be more precise, your flowers – have just dribbled water over my shoes."

"Oh no, they haven't, have they?" Glancing down at an expensive-looking pair of Italian shoes, she could see a fine spray of droplets on the leather. "Sorry, I hope it won't stain?"

"Don't worry, if it does I'll deduct it from your fee. And," he added quickly, "as you obviously have yet to tune into my wavelength, let me explain: that was a joke. Me being genial. An attempt at a little levity. Not, perhaps, the most original comment, I admit, but it's still early. Who knows, I might improve as the journey gets underway."

Kate looked back up at him. She sincerely hoped not. Saul the aggressor she could cope with. Just. But Saul on a charm offensive? Now that was an entirely different matter. Then it wouldn't matter which wavelength he was tuned in to because, whether she liked it or not, somehow those waves would always find a way to go straight to her heart.

As he stood back at the top of the stairs to let her pass, she wondered whether she should have put up more of a fight and taken her own car. After all, she was a free agent until Monday morning. And there was nothing in their agreement about pre-contractual obligations, which, as Kate watched him stride confidently round to the back of his Maserati, was probably just as well because she knew exactly who would have been responsible for the wording.

"I'd rather keep the flowers with me, if that's OK?" she said, noticing him reopen the boot. "That way I can try and control their dripping."

"That's not why I'm here."

Kate raised her eyebrows. "You're not expecting me to travel in there?"

Saul laughed. "With all your luggage? You'd be lucky to find enough room for your shadow. No. There's something which needs to be said, which I probably should have said earlier."

"Don't tell me the trip's off?"

He shook his head. "I'm afraid your services are still required.

No. When we last met, I said some things, behaved in a way I shouldn't have. I... Well, I owe you an apology." He cleared his throat. "I apologise."

For a moment Kate thought she was dreaming. "Did you just say what I thought you said?"

"I, too, thought about sending flowers – not stocks, but sweet peas. You see. I remembered how much you liked them, but I know you. Whether you like it or not, I *do* know you, and I knew you'd probably give them away or bin them. And then I remembered the picture in the exhibition which you'd spent so long looking at, the early morning Cornish scene by Tanya Morris." He put his hand to one side of the boot and pulled out a package, a small rectangular shape covered in brown paper. "Not quite so easy to throw in a bin."

"Oh, Saul, I couldn't...no..." Kate felt her knees go quite weak at this unexpected gesture, this act of kindness. "It's really quite... But I couldn't."

He looked slightly taken aback. "It doesn't come with any strings attached, apart from the one you'll need to hang it up with. I'm still planning to pay you, so you don't need to worry about that. And," he added quickly, "this is a business trip, so you don't need to view it as part of a grand scheme of seduction."

Kate flushed, and hated herself for doing so.

"It would please me if you would accept it."

How could she protest? She knew she ought to. She ought to throw it back in his face and tell him exactly where he could put it, but she couldn't. As she saw those long-forgotten traces of vulnerability in his eyes, she knew that was no longer an option.

"If it makes you happy," she began cautiously, "I will accept it. Perhaps you can put it with my luggage on my side of the boot, if there's room?"

"Not in the flat?"

Kate shook her head and prayed he wouldn't ask her to explain, as she was having enough problems explaining it to herself. All she knew was that the last thing she needed right now was to come home to a permanent reminder of the man standing before her.

"I thought I could show it to my mother," she offered, to appease his curiosity.

Saul didn't look convinced, but he placed the picture in the boot all the same. "Why do I get the feeling that that's where it's going to stay?" he asked. "With your mother?" But he didn't wait for an answer. Instead he slammed the lid shut and walked round to the passenger side of the car.

"Saul," Kate began, as he held the door open for her.

"Yes?"

"It's important to me that our trip goes well. That our *business* trip goes well."

"I thought I said a few minutes ago that this wasn't a bribe of any kind?"

"I know. I just wanted to hear it again." Noticing his lips tighten, she stretched up and gave him a quick peck on the cheek. "Thank you…for the present."

And, as she lowered her face and saw a small glow of pleasure permeate from around the corners of his mouth, Kate realised, too late, she'd just done an incredibly stupid thing.

*

"I don't want you to think I can be bought," she ventured as Saul negotiated the North Circular, "because I can't. I shouldn't have accepted it. Really. You caught me at a weak moment…"

"Why do you do this to yourself?"

"Do what?"

"Constantly punish yourself?"

"I do not."

"You've been sitting there for over half an hour, worrying yourself into a frenzy over whether or not you should have accepted the picture. Then, once you've been able to drag yourself away from that dilemma, you've been browbeating yourself over that kiss. Am I right?"

Kate shuffled back in her seat. She wasn't entirely sure she liked where this conversation was going. "Can we change the subject?"

But Saul had no intention of doing so. "Just so we're clear then, like most males, I'm not averse to the odd display of affection, but it did not make me hope for better things. I bought you a present – a picture you happened to like – not because I wanted to jumpstart our relationship again, because, frankly, I don't think they make jump leads that powerful. No, I bought you a present to apologise for bawling my head off at you the other day. Also, for the record, could you stop fiddling with your fingers? It's distracting your chauffeur and, if you're not careful, he'll have an accident and start bawling at you all over again."

Kate looked up at him. "I'm sorry. I guess I'm just…"

"Nervous?" he supplied. "Don't be. After all, it's not that far to Cambridge and then you'll be free of me until early Monday morning." And he would have the whole weekend to curse himself for commenting on those delicate little hands. Now he'd have no excuse to allow his eyes to wander across to where that short black skirt ended, and his journey of discovery could begin. A journey which would allow him to slowly, oh, so very slowly, meander his hands under that flimsy piece of material, swirling against the sensuous silk of those stockings, gradually searing higher and higher, until...

"Look out!" Kate's warning flashed through his foreplay like lightning. Braking quickly, he just managed to avoid a BMW which had pulled out in front of him from an inner lane. "You were saying," she reiterated, removing her fingers from the sides of the leather seats, "that I had no need to be nervous, if I remember?"

"Well, I didn't hit it, did I? No damage done. Thank God. Are you OK?"

Kate nodded. "Just keep your eyes on the road and not on my legs. After all, didn't you say there weren't any jump leads powerful enough? So don't try and invent any!"

She tucked her legs back neatly against the seat and tried not to smile. So, he still found her attractive? Or at least, he still found women's legs attractive. Now she could spend the rest of the journey worrying about that, or treat it as a compliment. She decided, for once, to do the latter.

"What happened to the Aston Martin?" she asked, as he swung out to overtake the car which had punctured his fantasy.

"I had a disagreement with a tree late one night and the tree won." The Maserati roared effortlessly past several more vehicles before pulling back into an inner lane.

"I didn't know."

"There's no reason why you should. I asked Helen not to tell you. It didn't exactly make headline news. More like a couple of lines in the business press. *Saul Preston narrowly avoids late-night merger.*" He laughed at the recollection, his hands relaxing against the steering wheel.

"Were...were you hurt?"

"The great advantage of paying £140,000 for a car is that when you go round a corner too fast in icy conditions and skate across the road, the traction control cuts in and the only thing you come out with is a blow to your ego. Anyway, why all the questions? Don't tell me you've had a change of heart and are suddenly concerned for my welfare?"

Kate ignored the question and concentrated on the road ahead. She was finally beginning to tune in to his wavelength, and she wasn't sure she could handle the frequency. If this was what it was like after only half an hour in his company, what hope did she have for the next few days?

By the time Saul pulled off the M11 for petrol at a service station, Kate's stomach was complaining so loudly he suggested they stop for some breakfast too.

"You've gone very quiet," he remarked, placing a pair of Danish pastries and two insipid-looking paper cups of black coffee on to the table in front of her.

Kate sat down and, picking up the knife from her plate, cut her pastry in two. "I've decided it's safer that way."

"May I ask why?" He raised his eyebrows inquisitively. "Why you feel that way?"

Kate found nothing encouraging about his solicitude, though. She started to stir her coffee, keeping her eyes firmly fixed on the spoon. "Because," she began hesitantly, "that way I manage to stop myself from being nice to you."

"I see. And you would rather not be nice to me?"

"Yes… I mean, no. Oh, Saul, I don't know what I mean… I'm tired. I didn't sleep that much last night."

"Perhaps you should have gone to bed earlier?" There was an unexpected note of exasperation in his voice, which caused Kate to look back up at him. He was studying her with one of those inscrutable expressions she'd seen him use to great effect in business meetings. He would have been an excellent poker player, she thought, had he ever been interested in learning the rules.

"Not that it's any of your concern, but I've had an extremely stressful week."

"Culminating in a trip to the theatre with Tim?"

"And that's another thing. Could you please stop discussing me with my mother? What I do or don't do is my business. Not yours and not hers."

"She's only worried about you."

"So by discussing me with you, she thinks she's going to make my life better?" countered Kate incredulously.

"You're being unreasonable," Saul chided soothingly. "Helen just wanted someone to talk to. She's worried about the way you're pushing yourself."

"And whose fault is that?" As soon as the words left her lips, she could have hit herself. Because she knew exactly how he'd interpret them. And he would be wrong. She didn't work hard because of him, because of what he'd done to her. She worked hard because she wanted to succeed. To prove to herself that, although she kept making a major mess of her love life, she could be successful at something. But now wasn't the time to try and explain that little philosophical gem to Saul. Kate wasn't entirely sure she understood it herself.

Hastily unfolding the paper serviette, she wrapped it over the half-eaten pastry and stood up. "I know that you...that my mother means it for the best. It's just that I left pigtails and gymslips behind years ago, and it's time she realised that. I'm really quite grown-up now."

"I can see that," Saul agreed, leisurely leaning back in the chair and folding his arms across his chest to appreciate the adult version more fully.

Kate groaned inwardly, wishing she'd been a little more selective in her choice of words. She could tell by the appreciative line of those sensuous lips that she'd just been catapulted to stardom in some foreign X-rated movie with subtitles.

"Perhaps it would be better if we confined our conversation to business from now on?" she suggested, quickly trying to censor his viewing and break the spell. "And, before you say anything about this pastry, I *am* going to eat it, later, in the car, if I may, once we've got going."

"Something tells me," Saul said, standing up and rummaging in his pocket for his key fob, "I shouldn't have had the car valeted yesterday. But," he concluded, "if it makes you eat that damned pastry rather than preserve it for all eternity, then it will have been well worth the expense!"

Chapter 8

The journey to Cambridge had never taken so long. Kate was sure she could have driven there and back in half the time it was taking Saul. In fairness, it wasn't his fault there was so much weekend traffic already on the road, or an outbreak of speed cameras. It was just that she wanted this journey to be over. Since she'd outlawed any conversation that wasn't strictly business-related, there'd been very little conversation at all.

Her driver, on the other hand, appeared to be surprisingly relaxed. As patience wasn't one of his known virtues, especially when driving, Kate couldn't help but wonder why. Why he appeared to be quite so happy to crawl along, tapping the wheel to Adele's *Rolling in the Deep*, without the slightest hint of frustration.

Then she noticed where they were, and suddenly it all made perfect sense. They had just passed a row of old sycamore trees. A little further on there would be the *Hansel and Gretel* cottage, with its twisted frontage, sloping roof, crooked chimneys and dark leaded windows. Kate peered out of the window. Yes, there it was, and the garden was still overgrown, just as it had been when she'd first caught sight of it over three years ago.

The bastard. Why did he have to take her this way? Why couldn't they have gone the way she always went? No wonder it was taking longer. And where had her mind been during the last half-hour that she'd only just noticed the route?

She looked back out of the window as the first turning for Dittworth appeared before them. This was where Saul was planning to spend his weekend; a quintessentially English village with just enough inhabitants to field a cricket team. And just outside, looking down over the cottages it once owned, was a meticulously maintained manor house.

"For us," Saul had told her, once she'd agreed to marry him. "Your name is on the deeds. No more surfing the net for that ideal home when you think I'm not watching!"

And Kate could have hugged him all over again, if she wasn't so intent on trying to forget. How he'd bought them a house with actual wings! The western side of which dated back to Tudor times, and had an old stone hearth, the height of Kate and many times as wide. There were flagstone floors to die for, and upstairs, nestling in the bedrooms, were nooks and crannies just crying out to be explored.

And Kate had. She'd searched every corner she could find in the hope of discovering a priest's hole or, at the very least, a hidden passage, but the house had refused to give up its secrets.

It stood as it had since Georgian times, when they'd added to its floorplan, elevating the Manor to grandiose proportions, with classical style and structure attached to every feature. It was a dream come true, or so she'd thought, as she'd strolled out across the lawn, but dreams come at a price. Kate stole a glance at Saul.

And love him as she had, it wasn't a price she was prepared to pay.

She quickly wiped a tear away from her cheek.

"There are tissues in the glove compartment," he prompted.

"It's hayfever. It gets worse every year," Kate muttered. "It's all this rape," she claimed, realising, too late, that there wasn't a single rape field in sight, and hating him for noticing.

Saul began to slow down. "I can turn off here," he said, as they approached the second turning for Dittworth. "If you want to have a look?"

"No." She shook her head emphatically, searching in her handbag for a tissue. "No, thank you. I'm surprised, though, that you've still got it," she added, giving her nose a little blow before stuffing her hankie back into her bag.

"You thought I'd sell? I thought about it. Why keep a house that size when there's just me? But then you don't know what the future may bring, do you? There might come a time when there's more than just me. And it would be a great place to bring up kids."

"And...and is there a future Mrs Preston on the horizon?" She hated herself for asking, but couldn't help it. "I just wondered whether Hatti—"

"Patti."

"Sorry, Patti was destined for the Manor?"

Saul looked, to Kate's surprise, as though he were about to burst out laughing. "Do I take it you wouldn't approve of my girlfriend taking up the role of Lady of the Manor?"

"Oh, Saul," she protested in mock horror, not entirely sure why he seemed to find the prospect so amusing, "it's not for me to say who you can or cannot take back there."

"That's not actually true."

"I'm sorry?"

"Your solicitor was surprisingly lax in his persistence. I told him I would deal with the paperwork, with your request to gift me your share, when I got back from Germany."

"And you never did?"

Saul shook his head. "Probably still on my desk."

"For three years?" Kate queried, quietly cursing herself for not following through on this, for assuming that everything was in place. "And in all that time, you never thought about dealing with this – not once? Why?"

There was a long pause, during which Saul appeared to consider the question. Once or twice, Kate felt he might actually answer it. But when he didn't, and she could no longer stand the suspense, she prompted his memory. "Saul? Why didn't you sort this out?"

"Probably for the same reason you didn't," he said finally, keeping his eyes fixed firmly on the road ahead. "We both had other priorities. OK? Now, if you could refrain from cross-examining me for five minutes, I'd be grateful if we could get back to business."

And before Kate could respond and tell him that nothing would give her greater pleasure, she found herself being instructed to check her emails.

"I've sent you some documents," he was saying, "which I want you to read before our meeting with Alicia on Tuesday. If you have any queries, contact me and we can sort them out. And Kate," he added, as she dived into her bag for her iPhone, "you can stop worrying. Only another fifteen minutes and we should be at your mother's."

*

91

Stop worrying? Kate picked up one of Helen's homemade scones before putting it down again. What was the man on about? How could she stop worrying? He'd thrust his company on her more times in the last seven days than he had in the whole of the past three years. And in less than forty-eight hours' time…

"Kate?"

…it was going to get a whole lot worse.

"You've not heard a word I've said, have you?" Her mother was staring at her from the other side of the kitchen table. "Look, my dear, if you're worrying about Saul being by himself, why don't you phone him up and ask him round?"

"No." Nothing could have been further from her mind. "Besides, I'm sure he's got plans. The last thing he'll want is me popping up and ruining them for him." She glanced up at her mother. Helen didn't look convinced, but then she didn't know Saul like Kate knew him. She didn't know of the existence of Patti.

"You've had the room decorated since I was here at Christmas," she said, desperate to change the subject. She scanned the old Edwardian kitchen. The mahogany units, which her father had installed more years ago than Kate could remember, were now a subtle shade of grey. The old Formica-style worktops had been replaced with rolled tops of oak, which also provided the trimmings to the various cupboards. "It looks really good. Grey is the latest thing."

"Is it?" Helen looked delighted. "I must confess, though, I did have a little help in choosing the colour."

"Oh?"

"From the man I'm not allowed to talk to you about, who gave you that lovely painting you've just asked me to keep."

Saul! Kate might have guessed. It was on the tip of her tongue to suggest her mother finally adopt Saul as her heir apparent, and disown Kate as the ineffectual daughter she so obviously was, when she decided to let the matter rest. The kitchen *did* look good, and if Helen enjoyed playing the helpless widow to Saul's man of many parts, then who was she, Kate, the mere understudy, to take it to heart?

It was only during lunch, when her mother had asked one question too many about her non-existent love life, that Kate felt she had to make a stand. If she didn't, she was in serious danger of finding herself miscast. And she had no intention of starring in a rerun of *Saul and Kate*.

"You remember Tim?"

Helen removed the salad bowl to one side. "The name doesn't mean anything to me."

"Tim from my office?"

"Oh, your employee."

"Well, he's a little more than an employee now."

"You mean you've made him a partner with Lydia?"

Kate groaned. Was her mother being deliberately difficult? "No, Mum, Tim and I are…well…you know."

The look of dismay on Helen's face almost took away the triumph of Kate's brilliant invention. Almost. But deep down, Kate knew this was the only way to make her see sense, and she had to see sense, for everyone's sake.

"Tim's really nice. You'll like him. He's hard-working, considerate and extremely intelligent."

"Next you'll be telling me he's kind to children and animals."
Her mother stood up. "If you'll excuse me, dear, I'll go and put the coffee on."

On Helen's return, it was as though the conversation had never taken place. "We're putting on *Lady Windermere's Fan* at Christmas," she said. "Did I tell you? And we've been banned from the Town Hall? No? Oh well, we have. Apparently our little productions lower the tone of the community."

Kate almost choked on her coffee. "They do what?"

"Oh, it's all to do with our last performance of *My Fair Lady*. Ted Bowers, who was playing Eliza's father, took his role far too seriously. He turned up drunk, fell over Mrs Rowbottom, and then was violently ill over the lead violinist. It made quite an impression with the Mayor."

"I should think it did," Kate said, unsure as to whether she should look indignant or burst out laughing. "Well, at least they didn't ask you for an encore!" She put her mug down. "Have you got any plans for the rest of the day?"

Helen's face fell. "I knew it," she said. "When you bought me the stocks instead of roses, I wondered, but now I know. You've forgotten, haven't you?"

Kate racked her brains. *Roses?* "Oh my God, it's your wedding anniversary, isn't it?"

"It would have been thirty years today." Helen produced a hankie from nowhere and proceeded to dab the corner of her eye.

"Oh, Mum, I'm so sorry."

Although Kate's father had been dead for over five years, Helen continued to celebrate their love as though he were still here with her. Every year she would dress up on the anniversary of their marriage, place a rose for each year of their love on his grave. Then she and Kate would go out to celebrate the twenty-five years of happiness they'd shared together, as well as those during which she'd only had his memory for comfort.

Last year Kate had been abroad and unable to get home. And this year, she'd been so wrapped up in her own world she'd completely forgotten. She had a lot of grovelling to do. And it started with a trip to the florists to collect some roses.

"Katherine?"

Kate was still grovelling several hours later. Only this time she was trying to locate her towels through a haze of steam.

"Are you still in there?"

Where else was she likely to be? Thanks to an antiquated plumbing system, the whole of Cumberland Crescent probably knew she was taking a shower. "Am I late?" she asked, reappearing and doing a passable impersonation of a beetroot.

Helen shook her head and followed her into the bedroom. "No, dear, there's plenty of time. We're not due at the restaurant until eight. I just wanted to check you'd brought that green dress as I suggested."

Kate nodded cautiously. Not only was one of her towels showing signs of shifting from its position on top of her head, but her mother was smiling at her like a Cheshire cat, which was rather worrying.

"You don't think the dress is a little too risqué for Othello's?"

"Not at all. Tonight's a very important evening."

"I know, but—"

"But nothing. Besides, we wouldn't want you not to look your best for Saul, now, would we, when he comes to pick us up?"

"Pick us up?" Kate squeaked the words. Or at least she thought she did. It was a little difficult to hear over the pounding of her heart. "What did you say? I just thought... Did I just..."

"Now there's no need to carry on so. You may not wish to associate with him, but I do. He's been very kind to me. He always visits me when he comes up here. In fact, last year, he took me out, while you were away again on one of your assignments. It wouldn't have been nice to exclude him this year just because you're here, now, would it?"

Yes, Kate screamed inwardly, yes, it would. How could her own mother keep doing this to her? Did she really want to drive her only child so mad that she spent the rest of her days in a straightjacket, rather than giving her a house full of grandchildren, because if Helen continued at this rate, that was exactly what was going to happen. Kate felt as though she were about to explode with such a range of emotions that it would be impossible to analyse any of them clearly without rewriting the rules of psychoanalysis.

"Have you never heard of loyalty, Mother?" Kate finally managed to utter.

"Yes, of course, dear. Now, go and dry your hair and I'll see you downstairs at seven fifteen precisely."

No, you won't, Kate ranted bitterly to the manipulated reflection in the mirror. Because I'm not going. See how she likes that. I'm twenty-eight, not eight years old. No-one can tell me what to do now, or who to play with. How could her mother do this to her after everything she'd said?

That was it!

"Mum, if I come out tonight," she yelled down the banisters, "I'd be really disloyal to Tim. Could you explain that to Saul, please? I'm sure he'll understand. And if he doesn't, just tell him I've got a headache." And if that doesn't work, she thought glumly, just tell him I've died.

"Don't be so silly, dear," was the rejoinder. "If Tim is as wonderful as you say, I'm sure he won't mind." And with that, Kate knew her mother's mind was made up. The subject was closed.

Chapter 9

When Kate heard the doorbell chime, she was standing in front of the dressing table mirror, slipping on her pearl earrings.

There. She was ready. Now she could face her ex-fiancé, and any of her mother's other little surprises, with something bordering on resignation. There would come a day, she reassured her flagging spirit, when she would make her stand. When she would, once again, be forced to remind Helen of her appalling taste in future son-in-laws. But not tonight. Not now she'd calmed down and remembered why they were going out in the first place. To remember her father, who'd once told her there was a man out there just waiting for her, who would love her as much as he loved her mother.

Kate glanced at her reflection and smiled. "You forgot one vital piece of information, Dad. You forgot to tell me his name."

She cast her eyes over the image in the glass and felt a certain sense of satisfaction. She was wearing her long black curls down tonight and, against the brilliant green of the dress, which hung just off her shoulders, they gave her an elegance and poise which she knew she was going to need.

She didn't need a man to tell her she looked good, but the moment she joined her mother and Saul in the hallway, she knew the additional time spent on creating her image had been well worth it.

"You look wonderful," Saul said. "Both of you." Although his dark eyes never left Kate, and she'd forgotten how it felt to be admired. How it felt to have that power of allure at her fingertips. And, as she accidentally brushed past him, and breathed in his proximity, she realised to her dismay that the attraction was not entirely one-sided. That she would have to be very careful else this evening might not go quite the way she'd planned.

Her little green dress was, in fact, just that. As she sat in the passenger's seat, even Kate was conscious there was more leg than material on view. And she knew exactly what effect it was having on the man sitting next to her.

She knew Saul was trying to listen to Helen telling him all about the new director at the theatre group, but his attention was with her, just as it had been earlier that day when he'd narrowly avoided crashing the car.

And when she leant across to him in the bar, while her mother had gone off in search of a menu, she felt herself flush with delight as she heard him catch his breath.

"You never told me about tonight," she murmured, her heart missing more than a couple of beats at this surprisingly frank appreciation of her assets.

"I didn't know about it myself until this afternoon." He broke off and slipped his finger under the top button of his shirt, undoing it, as though suddenly constrained by its proximity. "I'm surprised you agreed to it, though, knowing I'd be here."

"You don't have a very high opinion of yourself, do you?" Kate chided before glancing around the restaurant. "Have you been here before?"

Saul shook his head. "Your mother read about this place in the local paper and thought it might be worth trying." He paused, as though he were weighing up the possible ramifications of Helen's actions. "I think we should try and humour her. I know that given a choice, spending an evening with me would feature near the bottom on your list of desirable options, along with parachuting and deep-sea diving, but, since it obviously means a lot to her to…to…"

Kate could see by the look he threw her that he was uncomfortable with the situation. And, as his eyes lingered over her glass, no doubt wishing he hadn't offered to drive this evening. Then he could have shared this particularly enjoyable bottle of red wine with her. Poor Saul. A little wave of sympathy leaked out from under the barricades, taking her completely by surprise.

"What I'm really trying to say, Kate, and perhaps not as well as I could, is that for one evening and one evening only, if that's all you can manage, let's bury the hatchet? For Helen's sake?"

"Oh, don't worry," she reassured him, replenishing her glass. "I have every intention of humouring my mother. Just for tonight. And," taking another sip of the wonderfully rich wine, she added softly, "you're not as near the bottom of my desirable options as you might think. Who knows, by the end of the meal, I might actually be enjoying your company."

Several glasses later and Kate decided that she was not only enjoying his company, but also beginning to recognise Saul as a fellow human being. A distinctly attractive fellow human being, who just happened to be male. Which was more than a little alarming. And she knew she really ought to be concerned. Very concerned, because she was supposed not to like him. Not even a tiny little bit. But as she slid her empty glass in front of Saul's nose and waited for him to fill it up – something he seemed strangely reluctant to do – it didn't seem to matter. Nothing seemed to matter anymore. The pain, resentment and anger had faded into the afternoon, whenever that was. All that mattered was the here and now. And here she was spending this evening with two amazingly wonderful people, and now there was no more wine left in the bottle.

"When are you picking Kate up on Monday?" Helen asked, pushing her dessert plate from her with half a slice of cheesecake still untouched.

"Early. About five thirty. That should get us there in plenty of time for our slot. If that's OK with you?" The question was addressed to Kate, who nodded, waves of untamed hair falling momentarily over her cheeks.

"I'll be ready and waiting." She smiled warmly, wondering if he would kiss her goodnight. And if he did, whether it would be a proper kiss, a real humdinger of a kiss as he had at Maria's wedding, or just a gentle peck on the cheek.

"Good," exclaimed Helen, searching for her handbag. "Now, if both of you will excuse me, I'm going to love you and leave you."

Leave you? Sitting bolt upright, Kate felt as though someone had just slapped her with a wet flannel. What had her mother said? She quickly rewound the sentence, all thoughts of Saul's lips vanishing in the transcript. And then, when the replay was an exact replica of the original, and she caught sight of her mother beaming at her triumphantly from across the table, she wished she could put the evening back into focus.

"I assume that…that means you want us to stay here?" she managed to ask, not daring to look across at her ex-fiancé.

"Or go to a nightclub or something. The night is but young. Unfortunately, I'm not." Helen started to rise, and immediately Saul sprung up and moved towards her chair.

"I'll take you back."

"No, don't be silly. I can easily get a taxi. Take her out," she whispered under her breath. "Enjoy yourselves."

And with that Helen made an exit worthy of her role as the latest Lady Windermere, leaving her daughter feeling distinctly uneasy about her own part in this new scenario.

"You have to admit," Saul conceded, sitting back down again, "she doesn't beat around the bush."

"No," Kate gulped. "No-one could ever accuse her of that."

"At least you don't have to continue with this pretence anymore."

"What pretence?"

"Of liking me. She's gone now, we can revert back to battle stations."

"And…and if I don't want to?"

"Kate." He drained the last dregs of his one and only glass of wine, before banging it down on the table. "You and I have spent the entire evening trying to satisfy the wishes of one dear lady.

And for what it's worth, you've given a spectacular performance. If I didn't know you better, I would almost begin to hope…to feel that maybe… However, I do – know you, that is – and…"

He paused, twirling the stem of his glass around in his fingers. "Now she's gone, there's no need to pretend. You can abandon your role as the devoted ex-fiancée, because you and I know that that was not how we left each other this morning. And I'm too stone cold sober to believe you've undergone a miraculous conversion in the interim. Unless, of course, I've missed something here?"

Kate lowered her gaze, away from the question in those dark eyes. She hoped he wouldn't press her for an immediate answer, because she didn't have one. She'd had one at the beginning of the evening. At the beginning of the evening, everything had seemed so simple. She was going to prove to herself she could spend an evening in his company without hurling crockery at him. At the same time, she would show her mother, in the nicest possible way, just how wrong she was about them. How totally unsuited they were. And how, if the survival of the whole human race depended upon it, Saul still wouldn't be the man for her.

But now? Now the thought of saving the whole human race from extinction with the magnificent man sitting opposite her actually seemed quite appealing.

"Saul?"

"Yes?"

"Shall we make an evening of it?"

She thought for a moment he was going to choke. "You want to go on somewhere – with me?"

Kate nodded, her heart melting at the raw incredulity in his voice. "I haven't sampled Cambridge nightlife for years. It's still early…what do you think?"

He swallowed hard. "I think you're playing games with me."

"Why – because I'm not yelling at you? Because I'm suggesting that we spend a little longer together?"

"Exactly. I couldn't have put it better myself."

"And that's what's worrying you? What a silly man you are." Standing up, and discovering to her delight she still had perfect balance, she brushed away a couple of stray crumbs from her dress. When she looked back at him, she could see him studying her as though he were trying to rearrange the pieces and make them fit. "Are you coming then, or do I have to go clubbing by myself?"

This evening had certainly not gone as Saul had expected. When Helen had phoned and suggested this meeting, his gut instinct had been to say no. To keep to his original plan of waiting until they set off on Monday morning and then gradually try and persuade Kate that life without him wasn't worth living.

But no. He'd allowed Helen to sweet-talk him into agreeing and now, instead of hurling insults at him, or demanding he take her home, Kate was actively seeking his company. Something, somewhere, wasn't quite right. The question was, what was he going to do about it?

Opening the passenger door, he watched her slide gracefully down on to the seat. Then, as she tilted her face back up at him and smiled, a slow, sensuous smile, Saul knew the answer. Nothing. He would do absolutely nothing. And when he felt her casually place her right hand over his leg and begin to stroke his thigh, he knew he'd made the right decision.

"So where are we going?" Kate asked softly.

"Henry's."

"And how far is that?" Slowly her fingers trailed provocatively along the smooth fabric of his trousers, sliding seductively up and down, up and down...

"It's about ten...ten minutes from here." He could feel himself begin to respond, feel the need within begin to stir, and he knew he ought to put an end to this, that he ought to tell her to keep her fingers to herself, to remove them from his thigh immediately. "Kate?"

"Yes?" she murmured.

He ought to, but he couldn't. She was really turning him on. "I'm only taking you there..." He must concentrate, concentrate on the traffic, on the road ahead, on the traffic lights looming in the distance, "on one condition."

"And what would that be?" she asked in a voice which banished all future concentration to another hemisphere.

"That...that you don't drink anything else." He slammed on the brakes as the lights went red. "Not for the rest of the evening. I'm not being accused of taking advantage of someone under the influence."

Saul groaned. What the hell was he talking about? Kate was taking advantage of him, not the other way around. But God, it felt good! Those fingers, those wonderfully light fingers, as they swirled around, leaving delicious patterns in their wake. He glanced down at her hand. If she just moved a little higher, then...

He gripped the wheel so tightly that the whites of his knuckles began to shine through, his breathing becoming more and more ragged.

And then someone hooted, blasting the exquisite ecstasy of the moment away with a long, loud, penetrating honk. He glanced up at the lights. Christ. How long had they been green?

Swooping down and lifting her fingers, he dropped them back over her lap as though they were red-hot pokers. Then, with his foot hard on the accelerator, he sped off with his brain hammering away at his groin.

What the hell did she think she was playing at? A minute longer and he would have been lost. He wouldn't have been able to control himself. He would have had to pull the car off the road and show Kate exactly what he thought of that little five-finger exercise.

"You just behave yourself while I'm driving," he growled, praying she didn't notice the uneven nature of those words, nor the way he was having to fight to control his virility. "You keep your hands to yourself, unless you want to get us arrested."

"Sorry," she mumbled, gazing away from him and out through the window. "Are we nearly there?"

Henry's was one of the newest clubs in town, but watching Saul greet the bouncers, Kate had the feeling he'd been here before. With whom, though? Now that was an interesting thought. Then she remembered. Of course; that tall model with hair like Marilyn Monroe.

"Saul?" she asked, as he helped her to slip out of her jacket and exchange it for a ticket. "I'd like a glass of mineral water."

"I thought you might. Then, once you've found your legs again, you can dance with me until you drop. That's your punishment for that little charade in the car back there. That's if we can find any space. This place gets more and more crowded every time I come."

"Is that often?" she enquired, following him to the bar.

"When I've got guests at the Manor, it's somewhere to go on a Saturday night. Now," he informed her, handing her her drink, "get that down you, and we'll go and jostle for some space."

But Kate was in no mood to stand and watch. If she did that for too long, she might begin to sober up, and then she knew what would happen. Her brilliantly logical brain would ask her brilliantly logical questions, like what exactly did she think she was doing? And just in case she didn't understand the phrasing, it would conjure up lurid pictures of Patti with the legs and Claudia with the breasts.

And Kate didn't want that, because at that moment he was here with her, with Kate with the…with the…? What *did* she have that those other women didn't? She glanced up at the incredibly sexy man beside her. Of course. She had him!

Swilling back the cool, refreshing liquid, she handed Saul her glass, and slipped her arm through his. "Do you remember, at Maria's, when you said, 'Let's show them how it's done'?"

"I remember," he replied, raising a dark eyebrow quizzically.

"Shall we show them, then?" she challenged, pulling him towards the dance floor. "This time, though, I promise I won't make a scene."

As they secured a space amongst all the other clubbers, writhing away to the latest music, Kate glanced up at Saul and knew, with all the clarity of the slightly inebriated, there would never be anyone else for her. As the songs faded into different tunes, and the minutes spun into hours, she knew she was lost and, on this particular occasion, they could cancel the search party, because she didn't want to be found.

Whenever she felt his body slide across hers, whenever she came near enough to smell that evocative scent, to sense the passion, pure, unbridled passion she was arousing in the man before her, warm waves of love washed over her. She could hear his breathing quicken, as he drew her towards him. She could sense the sheer intensity of his presence, the warmth of his flesh, against hers, as the past swept her up and wrapped itself around her. She was his, in that moment of ecstasy, and he was hers, and that was all anyone needed to know.

Or was it? Kate flicked open her eyes. As if from nowhere a little doubt had resurfaced, propelled by a pair of heaving breasts. "Saul?" She struggled a little, trying to free herself as though that would help her to focus.

"Are you all right?" Saul murmured, releasing her slightly.

Kate strained to look up at him and met such a tide of undisguised longing that all thoughts of Claudia were instantly swept away. What did she care? What did she care about anything anymore? She was drowning in the liquidity of his lust, and nothing seemed to matter except that which was still to come.

"Do you remember earlier today, when we passed the turning for the Manor?" she asked. "Did you want me to see it?"

"You know I do. After all, it's yours too."

"Would you take me there...tonight?"

For a moment he seemed puzzled. "You want to go there?"

"Sometimes you can be so slow," she teased provocatively. "I want to see our home that never was. I want to see our bedroom. Will you take me there?"

"Do you have to ask?" And, cupping her face with his hands, Saul burnished her lips with such passion Kate was left wondering whether either of them could wait until they reached Dittworth.

"Go and get my jacket, then, and I'll come with you."

"Kate—" he began, but she quickly put a finger against his lips.

"There's bound to be a queue. I'll go to the ladies'. I'll meet you by the main door. You'd better go." Handing him her ticket, she stretched up and gave him a kiss on the cheek. "Thank you."

"What for?"

"A lovely evening."

"It's only just beginning." And with those words, so full of gentle anticipation, Saul negotiated a path towards the cloakroom.

Surrounded by shimmering white tiles, golden taps and Grecian columns, Kate wanted to break out into a song and dance routine from an old musical. She felt so happy. So deliriously happy. She was in love again, and it was such a marvellous feeling…such a marvellous feeling that…that…what was that noise?

Turning, she noticed a young girl sitting less than six feet away from her, trying to stifle her sobs with a disintegrating piece of tissue.

"Are you OK?" Kate moved towards her, berating herself for not being able to come up with anything more original.

The young girl tried to nod, but failed miserably.

"Can I do anything? Do you have a friend, perhaps, I can get?"

The young girl shook her head, her long blonde hair brushing against her tears.

"A boyfriend?"

That caused her whole frail body to contort with such pain that Kate wished she'd stopped with the previous question.

"Look," Kate said, grabbing some fresh tissues from one of the boxes and handing them to her. "Perhaps I can order a taxi for you, to get you home, if you don't want your…your boyfriend to take you?"

"I can't go home. They'd kill me."

Kate thought this sounded a little extreme. "I'm sure they won't."

"You don't know my stepdad. He'd do his nut."

Stepfathers were something Kate knew very little about. All she knew was that Saul would be waiting for her, and with him lay the promise of something wonderful. She couldn't, though, leave this poor girl here crying her eyes out.

"Sometimes things aren't always as bad as they seem, you know," she began cautiously. "Sometimes, if you talk things over…"

"What planet are you on?" the young girl asked, looking up at her through the eyes of a clown. "I'm bleedin' pregnant. My stepdad hates my guts, and my mum's scared of him. And now I'm bleedin' pregnant and my…my…" She started to sob again. "Doug don't believe it's his. And…and I love him…and he don't want me no more."

Faced with all this misfortune, Kate found it increasingly difficult to hang on to anything except the arm of the chair. This poor creature, who couldn't have been more than sixteen, with her sad tale and sorrowful eyes, had just sent her spinning back into the real world. And in the real world men frightened their wives, they got their girlfriends pregnant and then walked out on them.

And some even had affairs with their personal assistants.

Kate put her arms around the girl and gave her a huge hug. "It's all right," she whispered comfortingly. "It'll be all right. Trust me. It may seem like the end of the world at the moment, but it won't always be that way. Unless you're very stupid and keep making the same mistake over and over again. Now, let's see if there's a back way out of this building, shall we? Then we'll get a taxi. I'll drop you off somewhere. I'm sure you must have someone, a friend you can talk to?"

"There…there is Chloe."

"You see," said Kate standing up and offering the girl her hand. "I told you there'd be someone. There is always someone." A mother. A best friend. She sighed. Yes, there was always someone.

Catching sight of her reflection in the mirror, Kate felt that old familiar pain begin to stir deep down inside. A woman in love? Oh yes, she was definitely a woman in love, but she was not a fool. For a couple of hours tonight, she almost had been.

Chapter 10

Kate was awake on Monday morning long before her alarm sounded. She'd spent most of Sunday night tossing and turning, which was an improvement on Saturday night. Then she hadn't slept at all, but had paced quietly up and down her bedroom, until she'd run out of breath.

What had she thought she was doing? She was no better than Saul. And the sooner the pair of them became teetotallers, the better.

Yet it wasn't only the wine. If only it had been that simple. Then she would have awoken on Sunday morning to find everything neatly back in its proper compartment.

But she hadn't. She'd awoken to find she still loved him; that just the thought of him made her tingle all over with excitement. And no matter how much she tried to persuade herself otherwise, she couldn't. She loved the way he looked at her when he thought she wasn't looking. The way one corner of his mouth tilted just before he smiled. And she loved the way he seemed to genuinely care about her mother.

The only problem was, where did she go from here? Where did either of them go from here? There'd been no contact since Saturday, apart from a brief phone call to check she'd arrived home safely.

Helen had taken the call. "That was Saul," she said, poking her head around Kate's bedroom door to find her daughter in mid-pace. "I thought you said you'd shared a taxi?"

"Did I?"

"Yes, you did. You also said you'd got a taxi because Saul was worried he'd be over the limit. He didn't sound like a man over the limit to me. In fact he sounded very sober. And, if I didn't know better, very angry. Would you care to explain to me what you've gone and done to that poor man now?"

Kate wouldn't and didn't, because she knew her mother wouldn't understand. And even if Helen did, how could she tell her what had happened? That her only child had been about to indulge in a night of sexual fulfilment, when she'd met a girl who'd brought her down to earth? Who'd reminded her that with this love came pain? And that she wasn't strong enough to go through it all again?

"I'll explain everything in the morning, Mum. Don't worry about it. Just go to bed. Everything's fine, honestly, just fine."

In the morning everything was as far away from fine as it could be, but Kate refused to cry on her mother's shoulder. She knew by the way Helen peered at her over the cereal packets where her allegiance was. And nothing she could do or say would change the situation. Not even another skilful attempt at redrafting history.

"It was all so silly," Kate began, unable to meet her mother's gaze. "We argued over who should pay for the taxi. So I stormed off and got my own. Quite childish really, but there you are..."

Helen gave her daughter a disbelieving "hmm", but let the matter rest, which was just as well, as by now Kate was experiencing the first pangs of guilt. How could she have left him standing there? All by himself – without any explanation? What had she thought she was playing at? She'd half-expected him to phone and cancel the trip. She still expected him to do so some thirty hours later. And she wouldn't blame him. She really wouldn't, not after the way she'd behaved. She wouldn't blame him if he never wanted to see her again.

I'll give it another ten minutes, she thought glumly, staring back out of the sitting room window, and then I'll know it's all over, that he's not coming.

Five minutes later, the Maserati nosed its way on to the drive. Dashing through the hall, she grabbed the front door before he could ring the bell and wake her mother, but her foresight was unnecessary. She could see that Saul had no intention of calling for her. No intention of getting up out of the driver's seat, or acknowledging her presence whatsoever.

Tentatively, Kate walked towards the car. She placed as much luggage as she could carry by the boot, before returning to fetch her nebuliser. Only then did she hear the driver's door swing open.

She turned round. Saul was in the process of lifting her bags into the boot, and there, lying neatly folded on top of his own case, was her jacket.

"That's all," she ventured sadly, refusing to look at the item of clothing she'd asked him to collect. As she passed him her last bag, and saw him recoil from her touch, she was only too aware of the damage she'd done.

He didn't speak to her. He didn't even look at her. Having

placed the final case next to the rest, he slammed the boot shut and walked back towards the driver's seat. Kate wanted to cry out, to tell him how sorry she was, but the wall surrounding him was impenetrable, and she didn't even know how to begin to break it down.

The drive to the airfield was conducted in silence, Saul's gaze never deviating from the road ahead. When Kate dared to steal the odd sideways glance, all she could see was a profile, set in stone. No emotion flickered across those finely chiselled features, and Kate knew him well enough to know that it was probably for the best. That underneath this masterfully controlled façade was a man whose anger could be measured on the Richter scale, and right now she preferred the ground beneath her feet to be of the crack-free variety.

It was only once they'd boarded the Falcon, and Saul was no longer in control of any machinery, that Kate felt she had to say something, else she'd go mad.

"I'm sorry," she ventured, "for Saturday." She paused, waiting for some form of response. There was none. He continued calmly extracting his laptop from its case. It was as though she'd never spoken. "I... I said I'm sorry. I don't know what came over me..."

Slowly Saul lifted his head. Instinctively, Kate shrunk back into her seat. What was it her mother had once said? That underneath that tough exterior there was a man with a heart of gold? Not in those eyes there wasn't. They were as hard as steel and just as cold.

"You once said that all conversations should be limited to business, if I remember correctly," he stated tersely. "May I suggest you remember that for the rest of this trip?" And with that, Saul turned his attention back to what he was doing, retrieving the accompanying paperwork.

Kate had been dismissed. She felt as though she'd awoken to find herself in the winter of her life. There was no hope, no warmth, no love, only an agonising realisation of what might have been. And to make matters worse, she could feel tears well up inside her. Tears of anger, tears of despair, but most of all tears for something they'd both destroyed.

Quickly she bit her bottom lip and tried desperately to divert her emotions to other more mundane matters, such as whether Tim had remembered to tell Lydia about the new virus software, or whether her mother would remember to take her dress to the dry cleaners. But it was impossible. The man she loved had looked at her as though he wished her dead. No, worse than that. He'd looked at her as though he didn't wish her anything. As though she were as inconsequential as a speck of fluff on his trousers. She tried to smother an unwelcome sob.

"And don't start crying," came a gruff voice from across the cabin.

She looked up to find him staring at her.

"You deserve everything you get from me. Everything."

"I'm not...crying..." Hastily she wiped a couple of tears away with the back of her hand.

"Christ, Kate, what the hell were you up to? Do you hate me so much that...that you could... Is this your way of getting even with me?"

Kate caught her breath and shook her head sadly. "Of course not."

"Then what the bloody hell were you up to?" Stretching across to the table beside him, he thrust her a box of tissues. She took one, wiped her eyes and blew her nose.

"I got cold feet."

"Cold feet?" His dark eyes narrowed dangerously, as the temperature in the cabin dropped by several degrees. "Over making love with me?"

"It was a mistake, Saul. I should never have let it happen. I should never have let it go so far. It was my fault...all my fault."

"Don't be so bloody stupid. It was nobody's fault. It just happened. Or rather, it didn't."

"Sorry." She blew her nose.

"Don't be. It appears you did me a favour."

Kate glanced up, a cold shiver running along the length of her spine. "I did?"

"Believe it or not, I don't get my kicks out of waking up in bed the following morning with someone who doesn't want to be with me. Who would perhaps prefer to be with someone else?"

He broke off, and for the first time Kate saw the mask slip and the pain she'd caused break through. And she wished she could throw her arms around him and tell him he was wrong, that Tim meant nothing to her, that he was only a barrier, a decoy, to stop her from being hurt again, but she couldn't. And when she felt herself flush, which she knew he'd misconstrue as guilt, she watched in silent misery, as the mask slid effortlessly back into place.

"I suppose I should count myself fortunate you realised your error before it was too late. Only next time," Saul added dryly, "have the decency to tell a man to his face. It makes life a lot easier. Now, if you'll excuse me," he said, turning his attention back to his laptop, "I've got work to do."

And that was that, thought Kate unhappily. She didn't need a psychic to tell her that her audience was at an end, that she'd just been dismissed for the last time. Or that she needed to check her tear-smudged make-up. Standing up, she grabbed her handbag and began to make her way cautiously towards the cubicle, just as the *seat belt* sign flashed up.

"Where do you think you're going?" Saul's voice sprung out, causing her to almost lose her balance.

"I... I won't be long."

"Too right you won't be." Before she could reach her destination, he was there beside her. "You'll sit down, we're hitting turbulence. You can do whatever you need to do later."

"But I look a mess," she said indignantly.

"You'll look a bigger mess if you don't sit down."

"And if I don't?"

"Do you ever do what you're told?"

"Yes," Kate said pointedly.

"Then sit down."

"I thought you wanted me dead?"

The plane suddenly dropped in altitude and Kate reached out for support, Saul's strong hands steadying her. She could feel the power transfuse through her body as he held on to her, as though he was strangely reluctant to let her go.

"I thought something had happened to you on Saturday," he said after a few seconds, his warm breath brushing against her flushed cheeks. "It never occurred to me you'd stood me up. You should be very proud of yourself."

"Saul," Kate began, wondering if it was possible to feel any more wretched than she did. "I'm—"

"I know," he cut in bitterly, releasing her. "You're sorry. Now get back to your seat. Unless you want me to carry you?"

"I'll go," she conceded, "but I hope it won't last too long, this turbulence."

"Probably as long as we're together."

When Kate was finally allowed to undo her safety belt, they were thirty minutes away from landing at Palma, and she didn't know which part of her body to appease first. Never had she flown through so much rough weather. Never had she been so scared. She'd even considered risking Saul's wrath and demanding he cuddle her. That he wrap those arms around her and tell her she was being a coward. That the plane was built to sustain far greater stresses than these. And that the pilot had more flying hours than she had pairs of shoes.

As it was, Kate remained cowering in her seat until, after one sharp drop too many, Saul looked up from his laptop and took pity on her. "Kate, if you continue to act as though we're about to die, you'll bring on another asthma attack, and then you really will have something to worry about. So stop panicking and relax."

"H-how can you say that?"

"Because, although I apparently have a lot to learn about women, I know a great deal about flying a plane. There is probably more likelihood of being killed on the road out of Palma than there is on the plane going into it."

A possibility which was of no comfort whatsoever to Kate at that moment. "Do you think you could rephrase that please, without conjuring up the 'D' word?"

He regarded her quizzically. "You're really not enjoying this flight, are you?"

Kate shook her head. "Perhaps, if we survive, we could take a different route home – one that avoids the turbulent bits?"

She could see the corners of his mouth tilt. "I'll think about it," he said, as though that was actually a possibility. "Now, if you'll excuse me, I'm going to go and see Ted, our captain. See if he needs any company. You're to stay in your seat until those signs are turned off. Do you understand?"

Kate did, but she didn't want to. "Can I come too?" she asked as he undid his safety belt and stood up.

"No." Then, as though he'd finally sensed her genuine distress, he added with that hint of gentility she'd missed so much, "It's not like the other times we've flown together, Kate. Besides, I thought the last place you'd want to be would be with me?"

"Saul?"

"Yes?"

"Do you remember the first time we flew together?"

She saw him frown for a minute, as though he wasn't sure where this conversation was leading. Kate wasn't too sure either. She just knew that she didn't want him to go, that she would discuss the theory of quantum mechanics, or the evolution of man, if she thought it would make him stay.

"I remember," Saul replied quietly. "Although why you would wish to recall that trip is currently beyond me." And with that, he swung open the door to the cockpit and disappeared.

"I want to recall it, you idiot," Kate sighed, leaning back and clutching the side of her seat, "because it was the first time that you spoke to me, really spoke to me. And because, you stupid, stupid man, it was the first time I knew I loved you."

On their first trip together to Germany, the only turbulence Kate could remember had come after she'd been summoned to the cockpit. She'd worked with Saul long enough to know refusal was not an option. So, ignoring the infantile comments from Saul's purchasing team, she'd made her way nervously towards the front of the plane.

Once inside, everywhere she'd looked was covered with instrumentation of some sort or another, and there, sitting next to a bearded gentleman in a pilot's uniform and headset, was her employer.

"Are you actually flying this Falcon?" she'd asked, hoping she didn't sound too impressed.

"Not for the moment," Saul acknowledged, over the noise of the cockpit. "I've handed control over to Captain Harris here."

Kate smiled down at Captain Harris as he acknowledged her presence.

"But," Saul continued, "once we've had our little chat, I'll take over in time for our landing in Frankfurt."

What have I done wrong now? Kate wondered, as he removed his headset and turned round to face her. Ever since their first meeting, when he'd regarded her as a mistake, she'd felt he saw her as a challenge to his supremacy, which he could exert at any moment with those simple words "you're fired". And that feeling always made her more determined to stand her ground. That way, at least, she could always say she'd gone out fighting.

"Well, I'm impressed," she said, trying to ignore this feeling of unease. "I'd forgotten you'd said you could fly. A man of many talents. If you'll excuse me—"

"Not so fast." His voice stopping Kate in her tracks. "Do I look like an ogre to you, Bob?" he asked, addressing his co-pilot.

Captain Harris grinned. "Must be losing your touch."

"Must be. Because ever since I've employed this young woman, she seems to spend more time avoiding me than with me."

Kate was about to claim indignantly that that wasn't true, when she noticed the mischievous glimmer in Saul's dark eyes. "I can't very well avoid you if I'm interpreting for you, can I? And anyway, I'm not employed to have pleasant chats with you – not that I ever thought you were the type to indulge in such things – I'm employed to provide you with—"

"Has anyone ever told you, you look magnificent when you're angry?"

"What?" Kate wasn't sure at this point whether they'd suddenly lost altitude or she was no longer attached to her legs, because all physical means of support appeared to buckle from under her.

"Your eyes light up when you're annoyed, and the tip of your nose tilts upwards."

"Would you please leave my facial features out of this conversation?" Kate snapped back. Was it the confines of the cockpit or his proximity that was sending her such confusing messages?

"You see what I mean?" Saul laughed. "Any other woman

would have blinked and stuttered something stupid. But not this woman here."

If only he knew, Kate thought, if only he knew, praising herself on the surprising success of her blush control.

"All I really wanted was to get to know you, Kate. Find out how you're getting on, and before I know it, we're engaged in another of these crazy conversations of ours."

Kate felt suitably chastened. "I'm sorry. It's just…"

"Just what?"

How could she tell him he was having a strange and unnerving effect on her? That whenever they were together, the only weapon she could use to protect herself was her tongue? It was the only part of her body that still obeyed her brain.

"It's just that I was surprised you wanted a chat in a cockpit."

"We won't have much time after landing. And I've been meaning to speak to you for the past few weeks, but with work it's been impossible." He glanced across at his co-pilot, before turning his full attention back to Kate. "I really would like to get to know you better," he said, whipping her heart up into a frenzy with his glimpse into their future. "Everything about you: your friends… your family. But especially you, Kate. I want to know what makes you tick."

You do, she thought, bringing herself back to the present with a jolt. You made me tick then, and you still do. Though now, you won't even stay in the same part of the plane with me.

Chapter 11

As Saul drove out of Palma, leaving the Vía de Cintura and the city's various industrial estates behind them, Kate wondered if now would be a good opportunity to ask about the hotel. She'd followed him obediently as he'd marched towards the car hire desk; then again as he'd successfully located the vehicle in the car park. She hadn't wanted to upset him or the uneasy truce into which their relationship had fallen. There was a limit, though, to this mute subservience, and at least she no longer felt sick.

"I assume the hotel has Wi-Fi?" she ventured, praying he would follow her lead, and help put this trip back on a business footing.

He didn't speak. Perhaps she'd been a little too ambitious? Perhaps she should have gradually built up to this question with a string of pointless pleasantries first? But Saul had never been a man for the irrelevancies of life and, judging by the harsh line of that mouth, he still wasn't.

"It's not important," Kate persisted, not entirely sure why she was continuing to have this conversation with herself, "only if it doesn't, I shall need to find somewhere that does."

"You can stop worrying. The hotel is top of the range."

Encouraged, Kate continued, "Is it near the sea?"

"Not far, but I don't think the sea's visible from the hotel. There's a large swimming pool though, if that answers your question."

She could tell by the sound of his voice, the choice of his words, that he wasn't finding this easy, that he was making a supreme effort to try and come back from the edge, and she loved him all the more for it.

He began to fiddle with one of the dials to his right. "I'm not sure about this air conditioning. I'll phone up the rental company when we get to the hotel and get the car changed. If I keep it like this, is it too much for your lungs?"

Kate shook her head sadly. Perhaps silence, after all, was still preferable. At least that way she could protect herself from the concern in his voice.

Turning away, she peered out of the passenger window. The sun-beaten fields of the Majorcan countryside lay all around, dotted with the gnarled trunks of olive trees, groves of fragrant oranges and orchards of figs. When they entered a hamlet, they were mainly deserted, their inhabitants safely shuttered away from the midday heat in their honeycombed houses. Occasionally, a stray animal would emerge from the shadows and then slowly loll its way back to the shade, before flopping in a doorway somewhere.

Once they encountered a small group of elderly men, clustered under the shade of the trees, wizened by age and the sun, watching the world go slowly by. They looked so relaxed, so natural, so much a part of a life without time. Kate swallowed quickly. The contrast couldn't have been more acute, or painful.

She looked away and focused instead on the mountains looming in the distance. Saul had just negotiated a sharp bend, and the road was now leaving the flat plains of the south to begin its dizzy climb towards those peaks.

"I'd forgotten you suffer from vertigo," Saul remarked as she shuffled towards the middle of the car, and towards him.

"I do not," Kate began defensively, trying to ignore the increasing altitude on her right. "I just feel happier, at moments like these, if the weight is concentrated in the middle, that's all. Sorry," she added, realising that in moving closer, she was impeding his smooth gear change.

"I don't wish to disillusion you," he informed her, in a voice that told her he was going to do exactly that, "but I think you're a little confused. We would need to be hanging over a cliff before your weight would make any difference to this car's ability to remain on the road."

Kate groaned. Why did he have to bring up that scenario? Abseiling off cliffs was almost on a par with being jettisoned from planes at 35,000 feet. "Do you remember what you said on the plane – that there was more risk of being killed on the road going out of Palma than up in the sky?" she ventured, yanking her skirt out of his way. "Now is the time to tell me you lied and that I'm far safer on the ground." She peered out and quickly wished she hadn't. "Wherever that is."

To her astonishment, Saul didn't come back at her with one of his cutting ripostes. Nor did he lapse into a monosyllabic response. Instead, once the road had levelled out a little, he slipped an arm around her shoulder and gave her a surprisingly affectionate hug.

*

Kate was still mulling over this quixotic gesture half an hour later. Did this mean she'd been forgiven? Or had he become confused and thought she was Patti? It was something they probably needed to discuss, but now wasn't the time. Now was the time to intercede on behalf of a beleaguered receptionist, who was on the point of hoisting a white flag.

"What's the matter?" Kate asked, moving quickly across the mezzanine floor towards them.

Saul swung round to face her, trying unsuccessfully to hide his exasperation. "It appears that there's been a small problem with our booking."

"How small exactly?"

"My very clear request for two separate rooms has materialised into one double. With a double bed."

Kate felt as though her jaw had just touched her toes. That was not small. That was not small by anyone's standards. "And why," she managed to gasp, "would anyone do that?"

"Because they thought we were married."

"*Married?* What? How? Why?" Kate could think of a million questions, all hurtling at her at breakneck speed. What she needed now was some answers. She glanced up at Saul. His frustration was palpable, and in other circumstances, she might have felt insulted that the man she loved didn't want to spend the night with her, but in this instance, she was grateful. She didn't want to spend the night with him either.

"Your surnames," the small, spindly man at the other side of the desk offered by way of explanation. "Preston, Fenton – they are most similar."

"But they are *not* the same," Saul spelt out before Kate could. "If they were, if we were married, I would have asked for a double. I did not. I asked for two singles."

"Ah." The receptionist beamed up at him, as though he had suddenly seen the light. "You want two singles? The beds. You can move them apart. They are singles too!"

Just the thought of beds made Kate's knees go week. "Don't you have any spare rooms?" she asked in desperation. "Or," as the receptionist shook his head, "other hotels – there must be other hotels in the area?"

"We are the best in the area, señorita. And besides, the hotel in the next town will be full too. There is a very important wedding taking place."

The irony of which was not lost on Kate. "But I'm not married," she moaned. "And I can't share with you." She glanced up at Saul. "I'm sorry, but I just can't."

He held her eyes for a second too long, before he turned away and spoke to the receptionist. "You see my companion's reaction. You have two minutes to suggest an alternative, before I demand to see the manager."

"We have two guests still to arrive," the receptionist offered, frantically checking his computer screen. "From America," he added as though he felt the need to back up his assertion with some kind of proof.

Saul didn't look convinced. "Names?" he queried. Then, when he could see he wasn't going to get any, that it was more than the poor man's job was worth to divulge any further information, he pulled the computer screen towards him. "A Mr Jeremiah

Oppenshaw, it appears, and a Ms Shelly Oppenshaw."

"They have two rooms," the receptionist began, trying to reassert his authority, or at least regain control of the screen. "Two separate rooms," he added quickly, as though to point out they could get some things right. "I could book you or the señorita into one of them – if they do not arrive today?"

It was a long shot, even Kate could see that, but it was the only shot they had. How could she share with Saul after last Saturday? How could she lie just feet away from him, knowing what she now knew? And in the knowledge he found the thought of sharing with her just as abhorrent?

She turned to talk to Saul, to ask him to consider the possibility, when she felt the room begin to sway. It must be the constant change in temperature, she thought frantically, or the aftermath of the flight. One minute there was the blazing heat of the world outside, and then air conditioning that attempted to suck the lining out of her lungs. Neither were doing her any favours, as she tried to focus, to shake off the feeling of muzziness, but it was of no use. Reality was slowly something which was happening all around her. She was no longer a part of it. If she tried to speak, they wouldn't hear her. If she raised a hand to break out of this woolly cocoon, no-one would see her. She was part of another world, a parallel universe, where she was being compelled to watch her destiny being decided, but no longer able to influence the outcome.

She opened her mouth to try and cry out, but no sound came. In the rapidly descending haze, she was only just aware of the receptionist quickly drawing Saul's attention to her plight, of the brief comfort as he spun round, his eyes devoid of all emotion except concern.

"Kate? Christ, Kate, what…"

But it was too late. A darkness had descended, drawing a heavy veil over the rest of the world, and all, at last, was peace.

When Kate came round, she was lying on a double bed in a room reflecting the history of the island. Moorish arches lent an inner calm to the room, providing a dignified setting for the antique furniture that surrounded her.

Saul was standing by one of two equally impressive Baroque wardrobes. He was talking, in hushed tones, to a dark-haired gentleman of about half his height, sporting a moustache reminiscent of the artist Salvador Dalí.

Kate tried to lift her head off the pillow, but it felt so heavy, so out of proportion with the rest of her body, that she gave up. "Saul?" she murmured from her horizontal position.

He was across the floor within seconds. "So you finally decided to join us?" Crouching down beside her, he scooped up one of her cold, limp hands in his and gently massaged it. "How are you feeling?"

"I'm sorry," she muttered, not sure if she had the strength to meet his gaze. "I don't usually faint. Must be the heat…"

"Or the shock," Saul suggested softly, "of finding that the haven of two single rooms has turned into the hell of this? Don't worry, though," he added, patting her hand encouragingly before releasing it and straightening up. "I'm still in negotiation."

"Don't lose your temper, will you?"

"Why should I lose my temper?" He seemed slightly put out at the suggestion.

"You…you seemed so…so angry earlier."

"Did I?" He appeared to consider the possibility for a second before informing her she was not the only one to have been shocked at the news.

"Please don't make a fuss," Kate beseeched, finally managing to ease herself up with her elbows into a sitting position. "If the Oppenshaws don't arrive, then everything will be fine. If they do, then we'll just have to make the best of what's happened. After all, it is only for two nights…"

Kate couldn't believe she'd just said that; that she was actually considering sharing with him, after everything she'd voiced earlier, but she still felt annoyingly frail. The last thing she wanted was to be party to one of Saul's protracted boardroom negotiations on where she should spend the night. If the bed upon which she was lying could be split, and she had to share all this splendour with the man standing in front of her, at that moment she didn't care.

"I just don't have the energy."

Saul looked at her, concerned, but Kate knew he was not yet ready to concede defeat. "We'll talk about it later," he said in a voice that confirmed her fears. "You just stay there for a few minutes and stop worrying, while I thank the good doctor here for coming to see you, to check you're OK."

"And then?" Kate dared to ask.

"And then, I'm going to go down and find the manager!"

When Saul hadn't returned after fifteen minutes, Kate decided it was time to take matters into her own hands. Swinging her legs round and over the side of the bed, she placed both feet firmly on the floor and stood up. To her relief, equilibrium as she knew it had returned.

She wandered over to the balcony, relieved that the room was only on the first floor. The scenery was quite spectacular. Mountains, rising up against the horizon, stood in stark contrast to the seamless brilliance of the Mediterranean sky.

This was paradise, and as she located her suitcase, Kate had absolutely no intention of relinquishing it.

She was still hanging up her clothes when Saul returned.

"What do you think you're doing?"

"Unpacking," she replied soothingly. "And by the look on your face, I assume that you've not been successful, so unpacking really isn't such a bad idea, is it?"

He didn't look convinced. "I'll take my bags then, and wait in reception, in case the Oppenshaws don't turn up."

"And if they do?"

They both looked down at the double bed, at its proximity, less than three feet away.

"It comes apart," Kate said, as though somehow that would make all the difference. "The bed, that is. I'll call reception."

"You'll do no such thing," Saul said dismissively. "I got us into this mess, because I didn't check the bloody booking confirmation. I will sort it out."

Kate raised her eyes to meet his. "I know this isn't what you planned."

"It certainly isn't."

"But I don't feel too great at the moment. It must be the asthma or the turbulence..."

"And you want me to stay here? To look after you?"

"No. No, of course not. It's just…"

"Just what, Kate? What *is* it that you want? If I remember correctly, you told me I had to book separate rooms. In separate hotels, if need be. And now you're suggesting we share the same room?"

The tone of his voice told Kate what she already knew: that he was struggling with this just as much as she was. With a shrug of his shoulders, he sank down wearily on to a wooden chair. "And you think that's a good idea?"

"No, no, of course not, only…"

"Only what?"

"I don't think we have any choice," she finished lamely.

Saul looked at her as though he didn't know whether to applaud her for her logic, or chastise her for her naivety. "And what exactly do you think your boyfriend's going to say about all of this?"

"My what?"

"Your boyfriend – Tim?" Saul prompted, raising an eyebrow. "The man you almost mistook me for on Saturday? I'm sure he'll have something to say about you sharing a room with your ex-fiancé. Or aren't you going to tell him?"

"Of course I'm going to tell him," Kate retaliated, suddenly finding a burst of energy just when she needed it. "I'm not like you," she retorted, wondering how he, of all people, had the nerve to question her integrity. "I believe in honesty in a relationship."

"You're so sure you're right, aren't you? So sure that I'm a bastard – that I cheated on you? What I want to know, then," he asked, leaping back up on to his feet, "is why, if I'm such a bastard, you want to share this room with me?"

I don't know, Kate thought helplessly. I don't know why I'm so scared of being hurt one minute and then almost willing you to hurt me the next. I don't know why I'm accusing you of dishonesty when I'm still pretending Tim's my boyfriend. Or why I don't just give in, throw myself at your feet and tell you the truth.

Totally confused, she watched him stride past her, towards the door. "Oh, go on, then, go. Go and see if the Oppenshaws turn up. And if they do, I hope you'll be very happy in a…a broom cupboard or…or a bat cave…or anywhere else which isn't here."

He swung round to face her.

"I didn't mean it," Kate said quickly, just in case he thought she did.

"I know you didn't," he replied, with the briefest glimpse of a smile. "I'm going to check out the hotel's facilities. And Kate?"

"Yes?"

"Don't think for one minute I didn't try and change this, because I did. He's a very honest man, the manager of this hotel."

"In other words, he didn't like the colour of your money?"

"No, he damn well didn't."

Once outside in the corridor, Saul decided his examination of the facilities would start with the bar. Refusing to wait for the lift, he strode down the stairs two at a time, wishing briefly he was back in London and could rid himself of this excess energy with a couple of games of squash at his club.

Instead, he'd have a drink and then set about establishing where the nearest hospital was. This was always a wise precaution where Kate was concerned. He should have asked Dr Mendez, but his mind had been too preoccupied with single rooms and beds. Now, though, he was fully focused, which was just as well as he needed every grey cell he could muster, to work out how to deal with this unexpected fiasco. How he was going to survive sharing a room with someone who was not only pushing every button he possessed, but also manufacturing a few more of her own.

He'd thought he'd had it all under control. Her rejection on Saturday evening had certainly helped. Hurt, angry, frustrated and confused were just some of the adjectives with which he'd been battling since the early hours of Sunday morning, but he'd been deluding himself if he thought he could just withdraw. He couldn't. He was too deeply involved.

And so, he suspected, was she, despite her denials and the presence of this pesky Tim. Now all he needed to do was prove it.

Chapter 12

Kate couldn't believe her luck. After a surprisingly short stake-out, a couple of slightly overweight and highly bronzed sun worshippers had just vacated a pair of wonderfully situated sun loungers, under an even more wonderfully situated tree.

Hurrying across the terrace, the heat from the Spanish tiles rising up and seeping through her slingback sandals, Kate staked her claim. Now all she had to do was attempt the impossible – try and find some way to cope with the latest situation, before Saul came looking for her.

She'd been amazed when he'd said she wasn't needed, that she could have the afternoon off to do what she wanted. This was not the Saul of her memories, when every second counted, but Kate wasn't going to wait around for him to change his mind. Grabbing her mobile and puffer, she'd set off in search of solitude.

And now she finally had it, her own piece of heaven, perfectly situated under the clear brilliance of a Mediterranean sun. Stretching out under its shielded rays, she could feel the tension of the past week slowly begin to melt away. She would finish checking her emails later. She would panic about sharing a room with Saul later. But now nothing, absolutely nothing, would disturb this glorious feeling of inner calm, of heavy abundance. If only the person standing at her feet would stop blocking her sun.

Squinting through her sunglasses, she peered up. A dark, muscular figure of a man in shorts stood silhouetted between her and her supply of heat.

"You forgot this," the shadow informed her, holding out a bottle of some description.

Kate scrambled to sit up, as the magic of the afternoon ground jarringly to a halt. "Sorry?"

"Your lotion. You left it on your bed."

She took it from Saul and thanked him. The sight of her ex-fiancé, dressed in shorts and a brilliant blue short-sleeved shirt, had just provided the missing piece of this heavenly jigsaw.

"Why don't you stay?" she suggested tentatively, pulling her wrap over her lap. "There's a spare lounger next to me. You could chill a little."

"*Chill a little?*" He smiled. "This doesn't sound like you. What's happened to that hard-nosed businesswoman? The one who insisted on viewing this trip as a business proposition only? Who, even on the way up here, was asking about Wi-Fi?"

"I know, I know, but that's before I arrived. It's so beautiful here. Even you must agree with that!"

"If I didn't think it was beautiful, I wouldn't have booked it, would I?" he said, dragging the other sun lounger towards hers. "Do you want a drink?"

Kate nodded. "A long, cool lemonade would be wonderful, please."

When he returned, she noticed he'd ordered himself a beer. "You've decided to stay?"

"I'd finished what I was doing anyway."

"And what was that?" Then, when he didn't reply, "You don't have to tell me," she added hastily, "if you would rather not. If it's private or something." Her imagination had just conjured up a five-letter word beginning with P and ending in I, and she didn't want him to confirm her suspicions and fill in the blanks. "It's probably none of my business anyway. Let's change the subject. What time did you want to eat tonight?"

"Actually, it is your business what I was doing this afternoon." He sat down in the middle of his lounger and took a long swig of his beer. "It concerns both of us."

"I don't know if I want to hear this," she muttered. How she wished she hadn't forgotten her sun cream, and that he'd stayed in their room. But as usual, it was too late. "I think we should strike a deal, and only say nice things to each other for the rest of this trip."

"You mean you would rather we didn't talk to each other?"

"No, of course not." She was about to challenge him further when she saw him smile. "Oh, very funny. But if you're about to expand on the joys of your current girlfriend, I don't want to hear it."

"Who – Patti? Whatever gave you that idea? Did I mention her?" She shook her head. "I just thought…"

"If that's the best you can come up with, may I suggest you stop thinking?"

Kate peered up at him intently, and wished he would remove those sunglasses. As they both sat on the sides of their loungers and sipped their drinks, she was only too aware of how close he was. His knees were almost within touching distance of hers. And if she allowed her eyes to travel away from those knees, and along those sturdy legs, with their light matting of dark, wayward hair, towards those thighs, she could feel…

"Kate?"

…that all too familiar ache of desire.

"Yes?"

"You're not listening, are you? I said I've made a decision which affects us both."

"You're cancelling the rest of the trip?" She took a quick sip of her lemonade. "Well, that is certainly one way out of the disaster with the rooms."

"No." He paused for a moment, and Kate knew she was being critically examined from behind those dark shades. "Would you like to call it off? To go home now?"

She shook her head. "As you said, it's a business arrangement and if I go now, before I've carried out my part of it, I'll only get expenses, won't I?"

Saul laughed. "Now that's more like the Kate Fenton I know and…" He broke off abruptly, the contents of his glass momentarily providing a focus for his thoughts. "But we digress. No, I've made a decision about the Manor."

"The Manor?" Her voice was more of an echo than a question. "What…what has the Manor got to do with anything?"

"I've decided to sell it."

"I… I see." She didn't. At that precise moment she was incapable of seeing anything clearly. She felt as though a rug, of which she had been totally unaware, had been pulled out from under her, leaving her suspended in mid-air. What was happening to her? Until a few days ago she'd thought he *had* sold it. It had never occurred to her that he still lived there, let alone that she still technically owned half of it. Why, then, when he'd finally made up his mind to do what she'd thought he'd already done, should she feel the pang of loss so acutely?

"Why now – suddenly?"

"It's hardly been a sudden decision, has it? You, yourself, were surprised I still owned it." He took another swig from his glass, before placing it down on the table. "I should have got rid of it years ago. But I always hoped that maybe one day…"

Kate could scarcely breathe. "Yes?"

"That one day I would meet someone who would want to settle down with me and fill the house with kids."

"And?"

Saul gave a hollow laugh. "But I was chasing a dream. A foolish, romantic dream. Besides *Patti* doesn't want children."

Patti? Kate felt as though she'd been punched in the stomach. She'd thought they weren't going to talk about that woman? That he'd as much as told her she was stupid to even think about it? And here he was informing her, without so much as batting an eyelid, of their procreative plans for the future. What did he think she was – completely devoid of any feelings?

She swung her legs away from him, and snuggled back down against the comfort of the lounger. She needed time to think, to try and compose herself, only Saul had no intention of allowing her any such a luxury.

"As the transfer of title was never formalised, I need your consent. However, when you hear how much you'll make on such a deal, you should find that easier to give."

Kate wanted to scream at him. She didn't care about the money. She never had. The property had been purchased with his money, and she'd never wanted any part of it, but since he seemed so convinced she was entirely without scruples, why bother to convince him otherwise?

"What did the estate agent say then?"

"In the current market, and in its present condition, we should realise a figure in excess of four million pounds."

"Four million pounds," she repeated quietly.

"You see. You will be a rich lady in your own right now. Fifty per cent will be yours to do with what you wish." He paused. "You could even buy your Tim a new toy, a Ferrari or something for him to play with."

That was the last straw. "I don't want your money," she said, swinging her legs around and standing up. "I never have. That's why I tried to transfer title to you in the first place. It's yours to do with as you wish. Sell it if you want to. Move into a little flat in Mayfair with Miss Hatti...Patti Longlegs, if you want to, but just...just leave me out of it." Scooping up her mobile and puffer, she grabbed her sun cream and rushed past him towards the lounge.

But there was to be no respite. She'd hardly reached the lift before she felt his hand brush against her arm.

"You and I are going to have a little talk," he said, "whether you like it or not."

Kate did not like it. She did not like it one little bit, but there was no way she was going to have it out with him, there and then. Not, that was, until they were in the privacy of their own room.

Once inside, though, she could contain herself no longer.

"What gives you the right to talk to me like that?" she demanded, flinging the contents of her hands on to the chair. "To bark orders at me as though I were in the army?"

"Why don't you want me to sell the Manor?" He was standing with his back to the balcony, his hands slouched in his shorts pockets, his whole relaxed demeanour belying the heightened tension she could see all over his face.

"I never said I didn't want you to sell."

"Not in so many words. But I know you, Kate. What I want to know is why you don't want me to sell. And I have no intention of letting the matter rest until you give me a satisfactory answer."

Kate sat down on the end of her bed. She wished less of her flesh were exposed. She felt so vulnerable now Saul had removed his shades. If only she had the courage to go and grab something from the wardrobe, but that would mean moving closer to him. Definitely not a good idea.

"Well?"

"Well, what?"

"I'm waiting."

"Well, you can wait all day." Jumping up, Kate decided to risk it after all. She would be able to think better once she was wearing something besides a bikini and sarong. "You have no right to cross-examine me, Saul. I'm not on trial. I haven't done anything wrong. And I don't have to answer to you." She was now standing almost in front of him, but she was so angry, she didn't care. "I don't know who you think you are that you can still…"

But Kate didn't get any further. Before she knew what was happening, a pair of strong hands had disengaged themselves from their pockets and had seized hold of her shoulders. "I could shake you, do you know that?" he said, drawing her firmly towards him. "I could shake you until there is no breath left inside you, if I thought that would get you out of my system."

For a moment, Kate thought he might do just that, and wondered whether now would be a good time to tell him that she'd forgotten to take a puff of her preventative this morning. "Saul…"

"Shall I tell you why you don't want me to sell? Why you refuse to give me an answer? You don't want me to sell because that house still means something to you, because *I* still mean something to you. Sure, I've heard all about Tim, about how you couldn't sleep with me because of him, but that's not true is it, Kate? And don't look away."

Clasping her cheeks with his hands, he dragged her face back towards his, his eyes startling her with their intensity. "The reason why you left me looking like a prize idiot the other evening wasn't because of him at all, was it? It was because of me. Because of the way you still feel about me. And that scared you. That scared you so much that you had to run away. I'm right, aren't I? Kate? Tell me I'm right!"

No. No, you're not. You're so wrong. You couldn't be more wrong if you tried! The words kept hammering around her brain. But no matter how many times she tried to find her voice, to find some way of refuting this denouement, she couldn't. She couldn't because it *was* true. All true. Every single word of it. She *did* love him. She loved him so much that there was no room in her heart for anything else.

And now, as she gazed up into the depth of those eyes, all she wanted him to do was kiss her, to feel the gentle caress of those lips, the power of his tongue as it tantalised her with promises of what might follow. Raising her own hands, she laid them over his, the warmth of his flesh compounding that sense of urgency.

"Why won't you answer me?" Saul croaked. "Why won't you tell me what you want?"

"I want you to kiss me," Kate whispered, curling her fingers around his. "I want you to kiss me like you've never kissed me before." Slipping her fingers away from his hands, she ran them provocatively along the fine hairs at the nape of his neck.

"And then?" he managed to ask.

"And then we say goodbye."

"And if I don't want to?"

"We have to say goodbye, Saul," she begged, with a finality she didn't feel, as she tried so hard to protect herself, from making the same mistake twice. And for a few seconds, Kate wondered if she'd been too bold. If he would cast her needs aside as cruelly as she'd done his last Saturday. But he didn't. Pulling her tightly towards him, he lowered his mouth to where hers lay waiting. And, as his tongue furiously sought sanctuary, cajoled and caressed by hers, Kate had her answer.

So what if it was to be just one act? A beginning, middle and end, all meshing together under a Majorcan sun? That there would never be an encore? That she would never again experience the sheer scintillation of those fingers as they stroked her flesh, trailing patterns across her skin? They were together now and she would make this performance last forever.

"Tell me to stop, Kate," Saul implored, his breath warm and ragged against her cheeks. "If you don't want this, tell me now, tell me before…"

"I want this," she reassured him, fondly pushing his hair back from his forehead. "I want this as much as you do." Then, as a thought struck her, "I've got protection, if you need it?"

"I know," he acknowledged with a wry smile. "I saw some in your bag at the wedding. It's good to know Tim is allowing you to take good care of yourself."

Somewhere deep inside Kate groaned and hoped that wasn't where they still were, that when she'd transferred everything across, from one bag to another, she'd scooped them up too. "I'll go and get them," she said with slightly more optimism than she felt.

Prising herself away from his embrace, she staggered towards her handbag. To her relief, her fears were unfounded. "There you are," she said, handing over the packet of condoms and praying that the expiry date hadn't passed. "Although I'm a little surprised you don't have any of your own."

"Someone told me this was to be a business trip…" he began, and then he smiled. "Come here." And once again, he drew her towards him, his eyes this time ravaging the finely contoured lines of her bikini top. "Take that off. I want to see you. Really see you."

Undoing the clasp, her fingers trembling, she slipped the straps from her shoulders. Gathering the top up in her hands, she flung it away from her, her heart racing as he gently cupped those soft mounds of flesh with the palm of his hands.

"You're beautiful, do you know that? So very beautiful."

"Am I?" she murmured, feeling her nipples begin to harden.

"Very, very beautiful?"

"Do you need to ask?" Taking hold of her hand, he guided it down to where, in full arousal, lay the proof of his passion.

Kate could only gasp as the fire burning deep within her burst forth, sending flames of such exultation to every chamber of her body that for a second she thought she'd passed through into another dimension.

Prising his shirt from his shoulders, she began to run her hands over his flesh. He was hers and she was his, and this was the most tantalising feeling in all the world, as he scooped her up and carried her over towards her bed. As the sarong fell from her hips, and she surrendered herself to the magic of his touch. To the moment she'd been waiting for, ever since that night at the hospital, when he'd walked out of her life for good – or so she'd thought…

Entranced, Kate watched as Saul freed himself from his shorts and boxers, and allowed them to fall to the ground; intoxicated by the power she was exerting over him. Then, relaxing back against the cotton sheets, she waited, her pulse beating frantically, as he lowered himself down so that he was kneeling just in front of her. Stretching out, she tentatively touched him, holding him gently, her heart filling with joy as he pulsated with the pleasure of her touch.

Stooping towards her, he kissed her tenderly on the lips, before tracing a path with butterfly kisses against her flesh. Her breasts rising up to greet him, aching, yearning, demanding attention. Every sinew stretched to screaming point, craving to be satisfied, as she willed him to whisk her briefs away, to lay his fingers down where she needed them. Where she wanted them as she'd never wanted anything else before.

And she knew, as he raised his head to meet her gaze, as his lips paused in their exploration, that there would never be anything like this ever again. Nodding her acquiescence to the unspoken question, she lifted her bottom gently from the bed, while Saul lowered the material, evocatively drawing them over her thighs and down her legs towards her feet.

Having discarded the last vestige of her modesty, he raised himself up until their faces were almost touching. "I've missed you," he murmured, nuzzling her ears with his lips, "I've missed you like hell."

"Me too, I mean you," Kate moaned before grabbing his hand. "Touch me," she begged, "please, touch me down there."

He smiled, a long and sensual smile, before allowing his fingers to play with her inner lips, parting the skin gently and teasing her until Kate thought she could stand it no longer. And then he turned from her and slipped on the condom.

Lowering himself against her, he began to seek refuge, slowly enticing her body to yield to his persuasion and allow him access. This was heaven and hell all wrapped up together, Kate screamed to herself. How long could she stand this ecstasy, this – oh, such sweet torture!

As he lifted their bodies in unison, she drew him closer to her, holding him tight within. Her long, slim fingers running through his hair and across his shoulders. She could feel the tension in those muscles, the fine beads of sweat and the power of the man.

Did he do this with the others? Images of Patti flashed through her mind. Did he do this with her? Did she excite him in the same way?

Suddenly she needed to see his eyes. What was he thinking? Was that love or just lust? Oh, God, but this was wonderful! What did she care about Patti or the others? He was driving her mad, mad with desire. She wanted him. And she knew, as she heard his breathing become more and more ragged, that he wanted her. She could hardly breathe, but she didn't care. Every emotion, every desire, was screaming for fulfilment.

And then, when she thought she could stand it no more, a burst of pleasure shot through her, so seismic in its fallout that waves of contentment rippled continuously across every cell of her body. I love you, she wanted to scream. I love you, love you, love you.

But the words lay unspoken. This was to be their finale, their swan song. And when, a few seconds later, he, too, found contentment and relaxed back against her, Kate knew it was over. All that passion, all that love, just a memory to come. A memory that she knew would never die. Which would live within her, within both of them, forever.

Saul was the first to move. He swung his body over the edge of the bed and, remaining there, ran his fingers distractedly through his hair.

"I can't believe we actually did that. That you…that I… Christ, Kate."

"It's all right," Kate whispered, still basking in the mystical afterglow. "It's all right because it's goodbye." She trailed her fingers absentmindedly along the length of his spine. "And it... it was nice."

"Nice?" Saul swivelled round to face her. "Is that the only adjective your linguistic brain can conjure up? It was a damned sight better than nice. And it certainly wasn't goodbye. I'm not letting that be goodbye."

From far away, her brain lurched back into action. "What?"

"I'm not letting that be goodbye." He sprang up. "And I don't want to see you legging it through that door the moment my back's turned. I'm going to have a shower, and when I get back, I expect to see you lying there waiting for me. Unless, of course, you want to join me?"

Kate looked up at him, puzzled.

"In the shower? It will be just like old times. I could scrub your back, and you could..."

"Oh, no, no, no," Kate muttered, dismissing the image as quickly as it had arrived. "I don't think so, thanks. Probably not a good idea. Not in the circumstances. I'll just stay here. I'll be fine. Honestly. Take as long as you like."

The corners of his mouth twitched. "If I didn't know you better, I'd think you were trying to get rid of me."

"Who – me?"

"Yes. You." Saul leant across to where she was lying, and bending over, kissed her. "You won't get rid of me that easily, you little witch, not this time. We need to have a talk, you and I. And then, who knows? You may find," he breathed softly, "that the best is yet to come."

Kate lowered her lids, grateful that she was still horizontal.

It was less far to fall. What did he mean that the best was yet to come? Could anything be more perfect than what had just happened? Could she love him any more? Squinting back through one eye to check whether he was still within kissing distance, she doubted it. Nothing could ever match how she felt about him, or what had happened here today. Absolutely nothing at all.

When Saul emerged from his shower, Kate was once again engaged in another complicated battle of her own, this time with a sheet.

"It appears I came back at just the right moment," he stated wryly, surveying the swaddled sight in front of him. "Any later and you might have completely mummified yourself."

"Not a bad idea," Kate muttered under her breath. If only he would stay where he was and stop circumnavigating her bed. "I was just going to get dressed."

"Personally, I think you would look better in something a little more conventional, but then, what the hell. Be radical. Start a fashion. Or alternatively," he murmured huskily, coming to a halt just in front of her, "you could take the damned thing off and let me admire you all over again?"

Kate tried to edge away. "Don't," she protested, pulling the sheet even more tightly around her. "Don't...just don't talk to me in that voice."

"And what voice would that be?"

"The...the voice that says come to bed. Because I've been giving this some serious thought, Saul, while you've been whistling away in the shower, and I think – possibly – that this afternoon...on reflection...taking everything into consideration...may have been a mistake. Not," she added quickly as she saw his eyebrows knit together, "that it wasn't a very pleasant mistake. But it was still a mistake and...and I need a shower. Alone. Please?"

From the other side of the room, the telephone rang.

"Do...shall I answer it?" she asked.

"It'll be about the car." Unperturbed, Saul strode towards the phone and picked it up. "Yes? This is he."

Kate eyed the bathroom door longingly. Was this the moment when she should make a run for it? When, scooping up the acres of sheeting, she would defy the long arms of her lover, and collapse in a breathless heap on the other side of that door? Alternatively, she could make a run for it, he could catch her and she could collapse in a breathless heap on this side of the door. Not such an attractive scenario.

Either way, it was too late now. Saul had finished his call.

"You'll be delighted to know the hire firm has delivered a new motor," he said, replacing the receiver. "One in which the air conditioning works, or so they tell me. I've got to go down and sign some paperwork." He pulled a clean pale blue shirt out of the wardrobe. "Then I might as well go and give it a road test before dinner. Don't suppose you want to join me?"

Kate shook her head as vehemently as she could.

"I didn't think so," he said, slipping his arms through the material. "But don't go thinking that we've finished with this conversation, my darling, because we haven't. It wasn't a mistake, what happened here this afternoon. It wasn't a mistake any more than you walking into my office all those years ago was. The only mistake we could make now is to call it goodbye. And that can easily be rectified, so very easily rectified. If you'll let me?"

*

Flinging her clothes into her suitcase and then out again for the sixth time in little more than an hour, Kate decided she was just another pathetically spineless female. That she was about to set the emancipation of women back a couple of decades. And that her paternal great-grandmother would probably not have chained herself to quite so many railings if she'd known how weak-willed her own flesh and blood would turn out to be.

But it was no good. She couldn't go through with it. She couldn't walk out on him, even though she knew she should, that it was the only way of avoiding what Saul had planned for this evening's entertainment. She couldn't bear the thought of him returning, all alone, to find her gone.

Groaning, Kate slumped down on to her bed. If only she didn't feel so wheezy. She'd tried turning the air conditioning down and that hadn't made any difference. She'd then tried turning it up. The result was still the same. Further constriction.

She retrieved her puffer from the chair where she'd flung it, and gave herself two more puffs. Still no respite. This was not good.

Dragging herself over to her nebuliser, Kate opened it. One glance inside told her that if she'd thought the evening so far had been bad, it was about to get a whole lot worse. She'd forgotten to pack any ampoules of Ventolin.

She wanted to scream, but she didn't have the energy. She wanted to bang her head against a brick wall, if only she could find one. When would she ever learn? Asthma was not a game. It was not something she could outwit by sheer willpower, by pretending it didn't exist, any more than she could her feelings for Saul. She couldn't. It was with her for life. And if she didn't find a doctor quickly, there might be slightly less of that left than she'd hoped for.

Chapter 13

Fortunately for Kate, Dr Mendez was very easy to find. He was already at the hotel, attending another guest with sunburn.

"You come with me," he said, ushering her off in a wheelchair. "I have ampoules of Ventolin back in my surgery. Not far. Closer than hospital."

Normally Kate would have hesitated. Strangers and lifts were not usually to be recommended, not unless you wanted to end up dead. However, neither was denying yourself medicine in the middle of an asthma attack. So, with a muted apology to her mother for ignoring yet another pearl of wisdom, Kate accepted the offer. Clutching her nebuliser, she allowed him to whisk her away in his car, praying that he wouldn't take the hairpin bends at quite the same speed as Saul.

He didn't. Instead he ignored the road markings altogether, and more than once Kate wondered whether there was some divine conspiracy against her returning from Majorca alive.

To her relief, on this particular occasion, she was spared. Once inside the surgery, a rustic attempt at modernity, Dr Mendez set about rediscovering his sofa. Moving piles of books and magazines from a threadbare piece of furniture, he helped her to sit down.

"There," he said, inserting the contents of the ampoule into the medication cup. "I switch the machine on, you breathe in the mist."

Kate did as instructed, as she had as a child. Collapsing back against the array of cushions, she put on her mask and she waited for the drug to take effect. Little by little the pain began to ease. She wouldn't need to be rushed to hospital, at least not this time.

"Better? That's good. No need for steroids. Not yet, I think. You rest. You shut those pretty eyes and you stop worrying. I left message at hotel for Señor Preston. He knows where you are."

Kate wasn't entirely sure that was a good thing. The last thing she needed was for Saul to arrive and tell her what a complete idiot she was. She *knew* what a complete idiot she was. Only a complete idiot would have gone to Maria's wedding in the first place, let alone be talked into a business trip to Majorca, where she'd just spent the least businesslike afternoon of her life.

She let out a long yawn and pulled a rug up around her. Oh yes, she knew what a complete idiot she was. But it took a really special type of complete idiot to revel in the thought of doing it all over again.

When Kate awoke, she was back in her hotel room, tucked up in bed. It was after two in the morning and she'd very little recollection of how she'd got there. Just random snapshots of Saul bending over her, of strong arms scooping her up, and the faintest of protestations as he'd helped her undress, from a pair of trousers and a blouse into a pale pink slip of a nightdress.

"Don't worry, my darling," he'd reassured her. "There's a time and place for everything, and right now really isn't one of them."

She smiled. The memory of his words wafting over her, like a comfort blanket, securing her with their presence. She turned to thank him, for coming to collect her, but he wasn't there. His bed was empty. Screwing up her eyes against the gloom, she glanced across the room towards the balcony, at the glint of light from a laptop.

"Saul?" she called out softly. It was all she could muster, all she could manage, to try and gain his attention, but it was enough.

A shadow appeared in the doorway, a figure so familiar that she wished she had the energy to lift herself up and into his arms, but she didn't.

"You're awake? How are you feeling? How's your breathing?" Without waiting for an answer, Saul crossed the room and crouched down beside her, the faint aroma of beer mingling with the comfort of his aftershave.

"You came...for me?"

"I managed to get the doctor on the mobile. You were half-asleep," he added, gently removing a few stray hairs from her cheek, "so I carried you to the car and drove you back here."

"But," Kate began, still trying to make sense of everything, "you were late..."

"There was an accident. The road was blocked. I tried to phone you, to warn you to go into dinner without me, but you didn't pick up. When I got back to the hotel, I realised why." Pulling himself back off his haunches, he sat down heavily on the side of his bed. "You gave us quite a scare."

"I gave...myself...quite a scare. And...and you weren't here." She hadn't meant it to sound so accusing, but she was too weary to dress it up with finery.

"I know," he said slowly, raising his eyes to meet hers, "and I'm sorry. But Christ, Kate, have you any idea of how I felt when I got back here to find that you'd been rushed away, to God knows where? With a man I know nothing about? And all because of me?" He broke off, his voice beginning to falter with the strain of the last few hours.

Tentatively Kate stretched out her hand towards him. Seizing it, he pressed it to his lips and kissed the tips of her fingers. "Forgive me?"

"There's...there's nothing...to forgive."

"I can be so stupid, so bloody stupid at times. All my life people have looked to me, expected me to tell them what to do. You know what it's like, what my life is like. You've been with me, worked with me. And at times, I forget. I forget I'm not in the boardroom, that I'm not pushing through some deal or other. And I pushed you...kept pushing you...hoping...oh, what the hell does it matter what I was hoping? The fact is that if it wasn't for me, you wouldn't be here, struggling for air in some foreign country. You'd have been enjoying a quiet evening at home or going out somewhere with... with what's-his-name."

"Tim?"

"Yes, Tim. But it's all right." He paused, the furrows on his forehead deepening. "Because I've done some serious thinking. Moonlight and solitude, I can assure you, are perfect partners. And you're right. There has to be an end to this. It's making you ill, *I'm* making you ill."

"Saul." She squeezed his hand tightly. She wished she could think of something to say, something that would crystallise this moment into one they'd both treasure forever, but she couldn't.

"It's all right. I respect your honesty. Better not to say anything than to say something you might regret in the morning. What I'm about to say, I know I'll regret at some stage, but I'm still going to say it. I want us to remain friends. No, I'll rephrase that, because we never were friends, were we? I want us to part as friends."

"Friends?"

"More than that, I want us to spend our last day together in each other's company and damn well enjoy it."

Kate couldn't resist a smile. "Is that an order?"

"Yes, I suppose it is. Do you think you're up to it?"

Kate nodded, feeling the slightest tremor spill out from his hands, just before he released hers.

"You won't regret it," he said simply, "I promise. Now, try and get some sleep."

Kate watched as he raised himself up from his bed and walked back towards the balcony. Tomorrow was now today, and today they were to be friends. And she knew she should be glad. Glad that the strain of the last few weeks was finally coming to an end, that they would return to England and go their separate ways.

She knew she should be glad. But as a tear trickled down her cheek, she had never felt so alone.

*

When Dr Mendez called six hours later, Kate was busy trying to get herself up and dressed.

"You look a lot better, my sleepy señorita!" he informed her, as she wrapped her dressing gown tightly around her. "But you must listen to me. You must drink plenty of water. You understand? The sun and dehydration, it can be too much. Can make you very sleepy. Very dangerous. You must take care."

Kate smiled at him. "I will. I promise."

"And your asthma – your peak flow?"

Kate nodded. "I checked it this morning, and it was a lot better."

"Good." Dr Mendez rubbed his hands together and looked around the room. "Señor Preston, where is he?"

"He went down for a swim." At least I think he did, Kate thought, trying to recollect an earlier conversation. She'd been showering when Saul had poked his head around the door and muttered something about not being long.

"He's a good man, Señor Preston. He will take care of you."

Kate was about to tell Dr Mendez exactly what she thought of Saul's attempts to take care of her, when she stopped. Why did people always say he would take care of her? Her mother had never stopped extolling his virtues, and now Dr Mendez was doing the same. Couldn't they see that she was perfectly capable of taking care of herself?

"He was very worried about you, Señor Preston, last night."

"He was?"

"He wanted to take you to hospital. Just to make sure. But you were so sleepy that I told him, 'Rest, she needs rest. No more stress.'"

"What...what did he say?"

"He said it was all his fault. That he was the stress. That, after today, there would be stress no more. And then he lifted you up and carried you to his car."

"And that was that?"

But before Kate could push the doctor any further, and satisfy her curiosity, the door opened and Saul appeared.

"Ah," Dr Mendez said, turning round to greet him. "Señor Preston, I was just checking up on the sleepy señorita."

To Kate's surprise, Saul didn't appear overjoyed at seeing him. "When I left her, she appeared a lot better." He glanced across at Kate, seeking confirmation, just as the doctor's mobile buzzed.

"If you excuse me. Must go. I will check this evening. If you need me, you have my number, Señor Preston."

Saul nodded and waited until the door had closed behind him before telling Kate he thought Dr Mendez enjoyed visiting his female patients rather more than he should.

"Whatever gave you that idea?" she asked trying not to blush.

"When I arrived last night, his attitude left a lot to be desired."

"That's silly. He was probably just worried about me, thought you might upset me. Where have you been, anyway? I thought you'd gone swimming?"

"I changed my mind and had a little chat with the manager instead."

"About Dr Mendez? And would you mind just turning away for a minute while I slip out of my dressing gown and into this dress?"

"Such modesty." With a chuckle, Saul turned to survey the view from the balcony. "I hope I'm wrong too. The manager as much as told me. 'Dr Mendez has attended patients here for years and no-one has ever complained.'"

"Except you?"

"Except me. Can I turn around now?"

"Yes, on one condition. Could you zip me up, please?"

As she felt his breath, warm against the nape of her neck, she wondered whether she should have struggled a little longer with the zip of her pretty floral sundress. Just friends. That was what they were to be today. Nothing more, nothing less. And she must not forget that. Not even for a second.

"You don't think that perhaps you're being a little unfair on the poor doctor?" she ventured to suggest. "Just because he was here at the hotel last night, and you weren't?"

His attempt at a sarcastic sneer bemused her. "You're suggesting that I might be jealous – of him? Please, Kate, if you're going to insult me, at least insult me with something that's worth the insult." He strode over to the dressing table to pick up his sunglasses. "I wasn't going to trouble you with this," he said, swinging round to take up the challenge, "but since you seem determined to take his side, let me just remind you of a couple of things – as friends, of course."

"Of course."

"When I arrived to pick you up, I had problems waking you. Now you and I both know that that's not usual after an attack. You're dozy, sometimes, yes, but not that dozy."

"I suspect it was the heat," Kate began, wondering why she felt so compelled to protect her kindly doctor. "And dehydration. He said so himself. Not to mention lack of sleep," she added, casting her mind back to the weekend, "or stress."

Saul raised an eyebrow. "Possibly," he conceded, "but it could have been the medicine. Did you check what he put into the nebuliser?"

"Of course not. I was fighting for breath, in case you'd forgotten. And by the way, if he wanted to seduce me, or worse, why did he leave you his mobile number? And tell you where I was? And then insist on singing your praises this morning?"

Kate felt a little stab of pleasure as she noticed her question derail him.

"He did?"

"Yes, he did. So I think, just maybe, you've made a mistake. That you should probably be concentrating on thanking the man for saving my life, rather than accusing him of trying to end it."

Her triumph at Saul's expense, though, was short-lived. She'd expended too much energy. "I'm sorry," she said, slumping down on to her bed. "I didn't mean to… I know you meant it for the best. Thank you for being concerned."

"It's difficult not to be concerned where you're involved. I sometimes wonder how…" He stopped abruptly.

"How I manage without you?" Kate supplied, raising her eyes in time to see him retreat behind that mask. "That's what you were going to say, wasn't it? Surprisingly, I've managed very well. I haven't had as many attacks as I've had recently for years."

"Perhaps I should come with a government health warning? No. Don't answer that." Saul scooped up his car keys, and swung the main door open for her. "If you're ready, shall we go? We're meant to be meeting Alicia in half an hour, and I have absolutely no faith in the sat nav."

*

The route to Alicia Gonzalez's hideaway studio was surprisingly easy to find, thanks mainly to some excellent instructions from the artist herself, rather than the use of modern technology. The only drawback was the state of most of the tracks Saul was forced to drive along. A jeep would have been more appropriate, he cursed, as the Renault's exhaust banged against another hump in the road.

He glanced across to where Kate was still gripping the sides of her seat. "Why don't you shut your eyes?"

"And miss all this beautiful countryside? No, I'm fine as I am, thank you. Besides, if I'm about to be catapulted into the next world, I want to know when it's going to happen."

Saul smiled. "I could always shout 'now' if that would help?"

"By the time I reopen my eyes it might be too late."

He slowed down to turn left. "It's not easy being you, is it?" he remarked as the car bumped along another dirt track.

"No, it certainly isn't," Kate said, glad she'd forgotten her breakfast again, "but it's only for one more day, and then we can go home and everything will return to normal."

When they finally reached the artist's studio, Saul understood perfectly why Alicia Gonzalez refused to leave her sanctuary. Stepping out of the car on to the dust-clad stone path which led to the first of a collection of white stone huts, he could see a hint of azure in the background as the sea beckoned for attention, lazily filling the space between the sky and the hills.

"This must be one of the most chilled places on earth," Kate whispered, clutching his arm.

"You can certainly see why Alicia is so reluctant to come to London, can't you?" That was good, he congratulated himself – she was holding on to him and he hadn't reacted.

Kate did, though. She removed her fingers and apologised.

"Don't," he hastened to reassure her. "It's not against the rules of friendship to touch me." Or me you. Just the rules of restraint.

She looked away. "Do you think she's heard us arrive?"

"If she hasn't, she must be deaf. I think the car probably made more than enough noise. I'm only surprised the exhaust hasn't dropped off yet."

And there, in the distance, was the woman they'd come all this way to see. A tall, slim lady of about forty, with long, dyed blonde hair, and a face so heavily painted that it was a work of art in itself. In one hand she held a cigarette and in the other a tiny, shaggy-looking dog.

Saul watched, bemused, as Kate stepped forward and greeted their host in fluent Castilian Spanish, while the dog yelped its disapproval in a high-pitched squeal.

How did you get the damned thing to shut up, Saul wondered, as though there might be a convenient switch somewhere. If there was, Alicia had no intention of using it. She'd put the mutt on the ground before coming straight towards him. Unfortunately, so was the dog. Moving forward to kiss her on both cheeks, Saul soon found himself under attack. A set of sharp teeth had grabbed hold of his right trouser leg, and showed no sign of letting go.

"Bad, darling," Kate interpreted as Alicia scolded the dog.

"Excuse him, but he doesn't like men touching me."

Saul tried to smile, to brush it off, as though getting attacked by jealous animals was an everyday occurrence. "No problem," he said, resisting the urge to flex his muscles and test the animal's flying potential.

"You handled that brilliantly," Kate whispered, once their hostess was out of earshot.

"Another minute and I would have lost it."

"Just as well you didn't. Don't think Alicia would be too impressed if you damaged her dog. Now, follow me and do try and behave."

"I'm trying," Saul muttered under his breath, "but when you look at me like that, it's bloody hard."

He watched as Kate followed Alicia down an overgrown path towards another cluster of huts. In the last few years, Ms Gonzalez had shot to prominence and was now one of Spain's most promising new artists. Her landscapes, so rich in colour, texture and energy, provided an exciting new insight into the movement of the countryside. All Saul had to do was convince her the Grenville gallery was the best place in which to hang her work, and then this trip would not have been in vain.

He'd no idea what Kate was saying, but Alicia seemed to be enjoying the conversation, which was a positive start. He just hoped his interpreter's health would hold out. He knew he probably should have cancelled the visit and made her rest, but she'd seemed so much better this morning.

"Saul? This is Alicia's studio," Kate said, indicating the furthest hut. "She wants us to go in." Then, as he drew alongside her,

"I think she likes me. Am I right in thinking she's not very keen on men?"

Saul grinned. "Rumour has it that is the case. Why?"

"I just wondered, that was all." She waited until he'd followed her down some steep stone steps into the studio, before asking, "That wasn't why you brought me, was it?"

"No, my dear. I brought you for your language skills. If you also happen to be pretty and the right sex, then that was an added bonus as far as I was concerned."

"You...you underhand..." She broke off. Alicia was smiling across at them, holding a couple of glasses of lemonade. "All men are pigs," she said to her hostess in fluent Castilian, "don't you agree? *Gracias,*" she added, taking her drink and following Alicia into the middle of the studio.

Canvases of all sizes, hanging from every conceivable space, surrounded them. Against the cool white of the stone walls, bold flashes of colour conjured up spectacular sunsets, spilling over to wild and rugged landscapes, emblazoned with hues of indigo, blue, magenta and gold.

Kate had never seen anything so magnificent. "Saul," she croaked, "these are amazing."

"I know." He, too, was moved by the talent on view. "I want this exhibition, Kate. Go and do what you do best." Charm your opponent into submission. And then, in return, I will walk out of your life. But first, I will show you what we could have had. A day spent in the company of a friend, who wanted it to be so much more.

*

"You were wonderful," Saul congratulated her, as he tried to reverse an unwilling vehicle back along the mountainous drive. "Bloody marvellous."

"I know," Kate agreed smugly, waving farewell to Alicia. "Don't suppose it qualifies for a bonus? My extraordinarily gifted performance back there?"

Saul smiled. "Don't tell me, your new translation memory is costing more than you thought?"

Kate glanced across at him, confused.

"Something Lydia said," he clarified, "when I dropped off the invitation. Don't worry, though, I'm not insulted. I always knew it was my business you were after when you accepted the assignment, not me, personally."

Now Kate felt guilty. "It was never like that," she began. "Well, not entirely." But before she could expand and put forward a case in her defence, Saul had backed the car into a clearing and was showing absolutely no signs of moving it forward. "Is there something wrong?" she asked anxiously, her eyes darting from him to the car to the world outside. "Only it's getting a little hot in here."

"That's why I'm keeping the engine on," he said, turning up the air conditioning. But there was nothing, absolutely nothing he could turn up or on to cope with the heat she could feel frizzling away between them.

"If it's about my bonus," she said, frantically reassessing her options, "forget it. I don't need it. I was just being greedy."

"I know you were," he acknowledged wryly, as their eyes finally met, "but we need to talk, Kate, and I can do it better if

I'm not fighting with the steering wheel and rear suspension at the same time."

"Do we? Do we really need to talk?"

"Yes, yes we do, especially when I need to thank you." And before Kate could protest, and tell him that it wasn't necessary, that sticking to today's agenda was the only thing that mattered, he'd scooped up her hand in his. "Thank you," he said softly as he raised her fingers to his lips and kissed them with the gentlest of caresses, "thank you for everything."

There was no pretence in his voice. No guarded emotion. Just honesty. And it tugged at Kate's heart with a force beyond the pull of gravity. She loved him. She loved him so much that it was tempting to show him how much. To shower him with her own version of gratitude, in the cramped conditions of the car; but she couldn't. She had to stick to the plan, whatever it was, as though their lives depended upon it.

"Friends," she gasped, the warmth of his touch, of his flesh against hers, reminding her that there was only so much heat a recovering asthmatic could take. "Friends – remember?" Then, in case he didn't, "Do…do you think we should be getting back?"

Saul raised an eyebrow quizzically. "Are you in such a hurry to part from me?"

"No, no, of course not, but—"

"But nothing. How are you feeling?"

All right, she wanted to answer, or at least she had been until a few minutes ago. "Why do you want to know?"

"Because I have a surprise for you – if you think your lungs can cope? Then I promise I'll take you back. As friends. As very *dear* friends," he clarified, just in case she was in any doubt. "But first I want to show you something. Something which I think you just might like."

Half an hour later and Kate was glad he had, that she'd ignored every pretext for refusal and accepted his invitation. She was standing on top of a cliff, looking down at the sea; both feet firmly entrenched on solid, if slightly dust-strewn stone. Her arm linked tightly through Saul's, as though he were her anchor to the world.

"It's amazing," she enthused, as the vista before her, of Mediterranean brilliance, rose up in glorious Technicolor, and wrapped itself around her senses. She could hear the sea, smell the sea and, with the slight afternoon breeze, almost taste the sea. The mountains, in all their splendour, surrounding them, like guardians at a feast, with patches of green clinging to the rocks for their very existence. "Even better than at Alicia's!"

"We can get closer," Saul was saying, "to the sea, if you like? I know you hate heights, but I'm told there's a path, which leads to the beach."

"Does it have a rail, or a lift to bring me back? Because if it doesn't, I think we might have a problem, unless you fancy carrying me?"

Saul glanced down at her, bemused. "I think that might just be a slope too steep, even for me."

"I'm glad the manager recommended this place, though," Kate added quickly, hoping that her reluctance for mountaineering wouldn't be taken as disapproval. "And that he felt able to share its secret location with you, but please, please, please don't let go of me."

Saul laughed. "I have no intention of letting go of you, my darling," he assured her, "and I think we can forget about the path, too, after last night. However, I do have something else which I think will please you." Leading her back from the edge, he escorted her across to where he'd left the vehicle at the end of the track.

Opening the boot, he took out two chairs, two small parasols to clip to them, and a cool box masquerading as a picnic basket.

"Afternoon tea," he said, setting it just back from the edge of the cliff. "Not exactly scones and Earl Grey, but slightly warm water, I suspect, and squashy strawberries – what do you think?"

Kate could have hugged him. Her tummy had been rumbling quietly ever since they'd left Alicia's. "Perfect," she said, as she sat back in the chair and allowed Saul to wait on her, the parasols protecting them both from the heat of the afternoon sun. "Reminds me of the time we went to Wimbledon," she acknowledged, as he handed her some strawberries in a bowl. "Without the tennis of course."

"Bit difficult to play up here," he conceded as a dot appeared on the horizon, and a sailing boat came into view.

"She's coming to the opening," Kate mentioned, once she'd had her fill of the fruit. "Alicia told me as we left that she wants to be there for opening night. And she wants me to be there too. I know that's not what we agreed, that we wouldn't see each other after tomorrow, so I hope you don't mind?"

Saul didn't reply. And for a moment Kate wondered if she'd been too bold, if she'd succeeded in annoying him, in doing the one thing she'd promised herself she wouldn't do, ever since he'd told her she was wonderful.

"Well, that does it, then, doesn't it?" he said finally.

"It does?"

"How could I deny you a bonus now? I will have the artist as well as her work!"

And with a relief so palpable that Kate was sure it could be felt halfway across the globe, she gave out a heartfelt yippee. "Thank you," she said, as she held out her hand to him and they joined forces, their fingers entwined in the gap between the chairs. "Thank you for everything, but most of all, thank you for understanding my limitations and for never once making an issue of them. And for this afternoon. It has been just perfect."

Of course, Kate didn't voice these words, these thoughts of gratitude. That would have taken the relationship past friendship, and she couldn't do that – not for a second. She needed the label as much as Saul did. And so they lay unspoken, as they both stared out to sea, and the magic of the afternoon finally came to an end.

"I'm going for a swim," Saul said once they arrived back at the hotel. "Then possibly a cold beer, if you would like to join me?"

Kate shook her head, the excitement and exertion finally proving too much for her. "Don't worry about me," she said, as the manager caught Saul's attention. "I'll be fine."

And with an assurance from her that she meant what she said, Saul made his apologies and wandered over to be introduced to a couple of American businessmen, leaving her free to do the one thing she'd been putting off doing since she woke up that morning: phone her mother.

She'd lost count of the number of messages Helen had left

on her mobile. The last one had even enquired as to whether she should contact Interpol or the Foreign Legion. Kate smiled. Somehow she couldn't see the Foreign Legion being interested in the disappearance of one asthmatic interpreter.

"Hi, Mum, it's me."

"Kate, is that you? Well, you jolly well took your time. I was just about to put an advertisement in the national newspapers."

"Don't think that that would be of much use considering I'm in Majorca, do you?"

"This is no laughing matter, Katherine, I've been very worried."

"I'm sorry, but I did phone you when I arrived, and nothing's really happened since." She looked down at her feet. Any minute now she expected the ground to open and swallow her up.

"Could you be a little more specific?" Helen asked.

If she were about to be sucked down into the depths of hell, now would be an excellent moment for it to happen. Could she be a little more specific about making love with Saul? About spending time in his company and enjoying every magical moment of it? How did she get out of this without ending up with a nose as long as her arm?

"Mum, the hotel is wonderful. *Both* our rooms are wonderful, and the food is wonderful."

"And…?" Helen prompted.

"And we've decided to be friends."

"Friends? As in 'just friends'?"

"Yes. And to prove that there's no hard feelings between us, Saul's invited us both to the opening of his next exhibition. Isn't that great?"

"Kate—"

"I've got to go now. I'll tell you all about it when I get back. Love you. Bye." And before Helen could reply, Kate disconnected, and patted her nose.

Maybe one day she'd tell her mother the truth. One day, when the truth was a little less complicated, and she'd once again learnt how to cope with the fallout. Then, and only then, would she let her mother into their little secret. But for now, it was hers and Saul's, and theirs alone.

Chapter 14

When Saul returned to their room an hour later, Kate had just finished dressing for dinner.

"Am I late?" he queried, running his eyes appreciatively over the vision before him. She'd decided to wear the same little black dress she'd worn at Maria's wedding. This time, though, she'd draped a fuchsia-pink scarf around her neck. Her hair was pinned up, with just a few strands of black curls falling on to her shoulders to soften the overall effect.

"No, you're not late. I've got a couple of emails to send before we go out."

"So you thought you'd get dressed up first? Shame you're not linked up to Skype."

Kate smiled at the compliment. "Probably just as well, considering how I look some mornings."

Their eyes met and Kate could have kicked herself for venturing into the personal, and not keeping to the agreed agenda. "Anyway," she said, desperate to change the subject, "you seemed to be getting on very well with the two Americans earlier?"

He raised an eyebrow. "I was telling them about you," he

acknowledged. "How, thanks to your brilliant interpreting skills, Alicia Gonzalez is going to allow me to hold her first ever London show. And how I've got the very attractive woman opposite me to thank for that."

"Saul..."

"If you're about to query the validity of that last statement, I don't want to hear it, all right? Beauty is in the eye of the beholder, and at the moment I'm beholding you. Now, go and write your emails, and I'll have a shower. Then we'll go out and crack open a few bottles of champagne and celebrate our successes."

"Successes?" Kate queried, with the emphasis on the plural.

"Our new relationship?" Saul prompted. "Sure, we've had our differences of opinion," he acknowledged, remembering their earlier conversation about Dr Mendez, "but we've discussed them amicably without throwing knives at each other. And we've had fun, Kate – we've spent a day in each other's company and enjoyed it. Surely that's worth celebrating?"

She smiled. "I'm not sure drinking is a good idea at the moment," she conceded, "but a small glass of champagne shouldn't hurt. Go on. Go and get ready then, and I'll send these emails."

Kate sat down at her laptop to respond to her emails and was just about to press send, when Saul put his head back round the bathroom door.

"Oh, and by the way, Tim phoned for you."

"What – just now?"

"No. This morning, when you were in the shower."

"Why didn't you tell me? What did he say?"

"Something about a quote."

Kate jumped off the bed. "And you've only just remembered?"

"It must have slipped my mind. But I'm sure, if it was that urgent, he would have phoned back. Or sent an email."

"Not necessarily."

"And why's that?"

"Because he knows I'm busy, that I'm with a client." All the good will, good humour, good intentions, vanishing as she stared at the half-naked man in front of her.

"Where are you going?" Saul asked, as she quickly pressed send and headed for the door.

"To phone Tim in private," she said, clutching her mobile. "To apologise for my client's deliberate forgetfulness. And then, if the kitchen can spare them, to find some knives to throw at you!"

When Kate returned fifteen minutes later, Saul was showered, dressed and ready to go. If only he didn't look so handsome, she pondered, she might have been able to stay mad at him long enough to hate him. But she couldn't. In a pair of cool grey cotton trousers, pale blue shirt and dark grey jacket, he looked so distinguished that it was all Kate could do to remember why she was cross with him in the first place.

"All good?" he asked as she checked her bag for her puffer.

"With us or with Tim?"

"With Tim of course."

"Perfect, as always."

"And with us?" he added, just when she'd thought he wouldn't. "Only I seem to be remarkably free of puncture marks."

Kate smiled. It was impossible to do anything else. "I gave the kitchen a miss," she conceded, "in the name of friendship."

"I'm glad to hear it."

"But I'm not missing dinner," she said, in case he thought she might. "I've got a quote to work on later tonight for Tim, but now I'm actually hungry. Shall we go?"

Saul wasn't sure if it was the beers he'd consumed with the Americans, or his conscience pricking, but he had an overpowering urge to confess. To put things right before he found himself accused of anything else.

"I've got something else to tell you," he said as they walked towards the lift. "I met Dr Mendez this evening. He was on his way to see you, but I dissuaded him."

Kate gave him an anxious glance. "You didn't upset him, did you?"

"No, of course I didn't. I was very polite. But I did tell him he wasn't needed, that you were a lot better now." He paused, stepping back to allow her to enter the lift before him. "You are, aren't you – a lot better?"

"Of course I am," she said, with a certainty he didn't entirely trust. "You see, I told you that there was nothing to worry about, that Dr Mendez was just concerned about my health!"

"That remains to be seen," Saul muttered, wishing fervently he'd kept his earlier suspicions to himself. It was one thing for him to do battle with that green-eyed monster himself. It was quite another for the manager to bring it to his attention at their meeting that morning.

However, Saul had no intention of mentioning it now, and

letting it ruin their last evening together. So, with a mock flourish, he bowed to Kate's superior judgement, and following her out of the lift, escorted her towards the dining room.

This was what Kate had missed last night: the splendour of being entertained in a first-class hotel of exquisite taste, which simply resonated with the history of the island. The pristine white of the walls provided a worthy showcase for a collection of antique Spanish plates, each piece boasting pictures and patterns dating back to the occupation by the Moors, their colours repeated in the flecks of the marble tiles beneath their feet. And scattered throughout this palatial setting were tables groaning with dishes presented to appeal to every sense.

"See anything you like?" Saul muttered in her ear, as they passed a particularly pleasing plate of stuffed aubergines.

"Everything. I could eat everything!"

"Thank God for that, then. I can tell Helen she can stop worrying about you. That you do actually eat."

"Of course I eat," Kate retorted, thanking the waiter, who'd just drawn back her chair. "I ate the strawberries, didn't I?"

"I don't think that's enough to placate your mother."

"And that's another thing," Kate added. "Once we get home, would you do something else for me?"

Saul raised an eyebrow. "I suppose I should say that depends," he said, taking his own place at the table.

"Stop discussing me with my mother. I can't stop you seeing her. I wouldn't want to, as she seems very fond of you. And you never know, she might need some advice on what colour to decorate the rest of the house, but—"

"I didn't offer. I was asked," he interrupted quickly, before adding to the waiter, "A bottle of Dom Pérignon, please."

"I know, I know. But please don't talk about me. As from tomorrow we're to go our separate ways, so there's no need for you to worry about me."

"As a friend, though, I might care?"

Kate swallowed quickly, realising that she could be drifting off course here. "As a friend, I would be grateful if you didn't. Please?"

She was conscious she was being studied, that he was looking at her intently, but she couldn't meet his gaze. Instead, she placed her serviette on her lap, and began to fiddle with the material.

He had to understand that this had to stop, that she didn't want her mother to be hurt all over again. And Helen had to realise there was no future in their relationship, that there never had been, and there never would be. She wouldn't understand the concept of friends, which wasn't entirely surprising as Kate wasn't sure she understood it herself, especially after the events of the last few days.

How could you have a platonic relationship with someone you loved? Who filled your mind, heart and soul with feelings that you knew you'd never experience again?

You couldn't. It would be impossible. And so there had to be no contact. She'd honour her commitment to Alicia and take her to the exhibition, but that would be all. To be so close, and only be a friend, would be purgatory, and she couldn't live like that. But tonight, as the waiter poured champagne into their glasses and Saul raised his to toast her, she'd make an exception. Tonight she'd be the best friend he'd ever had.

Chapter 15

Struggling to unhook her little black dress, a few hours later, Kate wasn't entirely sure where it had all gone so badly wrong. How she'd managed to end up in their bedroom alone, while Saul had been whisked away to experience Majorca's nightlife without her. She was even less certain as to how she felt about it.

One minute she'd been sitting, listening to Saul's plans to sponsor impoverished art students, and the next she was gazing up into the faces of the two Americans from earlier that day.

"Aren't you gonna introduce us?" the blond-haired man asked.

"Pete." Saul jumped up and shook him by the hand. "Good to see you again. This is Kate, my...eh...friend."

Kate smiled, not entirely sure she liked the way the three men were exchanging glances. There was definitely a subtext here of which she was frustratingly unaware. Standing up, she offered her hand. "Pleased to meet you."

"Likewise. This here is Jeremiah Oppenshaw."

Kate turned towards a well-built, bearded gentleman and shook him by the hand. She was about to sit back down when she noticed two tall and equally impressive women totter into the picture.

"Just wondered if you guys wanted to go on out to a club?" Pete asked.

Saul glanced across at Kate. "I'm not sure…"

"Oh, go on, honey. It'll be a scream."

Honey? Scream? Kate zoned in on the female behind the husky voice. Why was that stunning redhead calling her ex-fiancé 'honey'? Had she, Kate, missed something here?

"Allow me to introduce my sister," Jeremiah offered. "This is Shelly. Shelly, this young lady is Kate Fenton, a former partner of Saul's here."

The two women sized each other up with the pugnacity of mud wrestlers. Begrudgingly, Kate attempted a smile. *Former partner?* How did the stranger know that? And if Saul was going to talk about her behind her back, why did he have to insinuate that she was a relic of his past? It made her sound more like a dinosaur than someone who was very much alive and kicking.

"Hear you've just closed one hell of a deal," Jeremiah continued, blissfully unaware of the sharpening of talons and spitting of blood. "That you've made your guy here mighty happy."

My guy? *My guy?* That was almost worse than *former partner!* Kate glanced back at Saul, who was talking to the redhead.

"Not shy about getting what she wants, my sister," Jeremiah observed fondly. "If she sees something, she goes right for it."

I can see that, Kate thought heatedly, watching the way Shelly was preening herself in front of Saul. This man deserves ten out of ten for observation. Only Kate wasn't ready to admit defeat. Smiling at the other woman, Pete's wife, she turned her attention back towards the architect of the disaster.

"Saul," she began, only to be cut up almost immediately by her new adversary.

"Do say you'll come, Saul," Shelly purred, sex appeal oozing from every expensively groomed pore. "We can talk a little more about that cute old house of yours. And I especially wanna know about the bedrooms, honey. After all, aren't they just the most important rooms of any old house?"

If looks could have killed, Saul and his new admirer would have been strewn across the marble floor, or hung from the nearest tree, or a combination of the two, with a third fate thrown in for good measure.

"Saul?" Kate tried again, trying so hard to keep her cool. "Is there something I should know?"

Saul looked distinctly uncomfortable, as though he was trying to resurrect his brain from the heavy onslaught of food, champagne, breasts and heavenly perfume. "I was going to tell you later."

"And what would that be, *honey?*"

"Jeremiah here is…hmm…in the market for an English property, and…"

"And?"

"And they – he – liked the sound of the Manor."

"Oh, *he* did, did he?"

"Yes." Then quickly changing the subject, before Kate could tell everyone exactly what she thought of that idea, Saul turned to Pete and Jeremiah. "Look, guys, Kate here had an asthma attack yesterday and I don't think she's up to an evening on the town. So thanks very much, but…"

"Oh, Saul," Shelly drooled, her beautifully curved lips fixing themselves into a full pout. "I'm sure Katie here wouldn't want you to miss out on all the fun, just because she's not up to it. Eh, Katie?"

Katie, or rather Kate, was at that moment cursing herself, firstly for leaving Saul alone with the Americans, and secondly, for possessing such an uncooperative pair of lungs.

Saul was right, though. She wasn't up to a night on the town. But she didn't want him to go without her. Nor did she want to stop him from going. She was having a crisis of conscience, made worse by not having a clue as to what he was thinking.

"Shelly," she began, "or may I call you Shel?"

"Anything you like, honey, just make it quick 'cause I'm in the mood for a little nightlife."

"Shel, if Saul wants to go, I can assure you I would be the last person to try and stop him."

"Then that's settled," gushed Shelly triumphantly. "Saul?"

"No, it's not," Saul interjected. "Kate—"

"Look, I'm fine," she said, wishing she was. "Honestly. I've got work to do. If you want to go, go." And for the first time since the beginning of this conversation, their eyes met; Saul's dark and questioning, and Kate's trying so desperately to hide her disappointment.

"Right, well ya seem to have got the OK from the little lady here." And with that, Jeremiah slapped Saul on the back. "Let's go get a cab. Though where the hell from, I sure don't know!"

And off they'd gone. In fairness, Saul had offered, almost insisted, he escort Kate back to her room, but she'd declined. She wanted to finish her coffee first. There was no need to wait. She would be just fine where she was.

And so he'd kissed her goodbye. Just a brief kiss on the forehead. The type given to former partners, to friends who were soon to go their separate ways, as all memories of this afternoon appeared to vanish. And then, with one last glance at her over his shoulder, he disappeared out and into the night.

It was after twelve when Kate crawled into bed. For Saul and his party the evening was no doubt only just beginning, but for Kate it was almost over. She was glad she'd not accepted the invitation; that she wasn't there with them. It had been a long day and she was shattered.

Leaning across to check her mobile, her only regret was that Saul wasn't here with her, to spend their last night together, as friends. Instead, he was halfway across the island with a woman whose idea of subtlety was on a par with that of Genghis Khan.

Why, oh why couldn't he have just said no? It wasn't a difficult word, and Kate knew it featured highly in his vocabulary at work. So why couldn't he have used it here? Was the thought of spending the rest of the evening with her really so awful? Or was it – and this was a bitter pill to swallow – that he actually *wanted* to be with someone else; someone rather than her?

Kate opened her emails and tried to focus on what Tim had sent her, but she couldn't. Events of the last two days kept flicking back and forth across her thoughts, like a favourite film. There'd been sex. There'd been love and so many different emotions in between, that when Saul had raised his glass and toasted her, when he'd held her in his gaze, Kate had almost believed there was hope; that she was part of his life again. His past and his future, as he regaled her with tales of his youth, of his plans for the gallery, and she never wanted it to end. She wanted it to go on and on and on, until, finally, she fell back exhausted and allowed her eyes to close. It had all seemed so simple once. Once, a very long time ago.

It was several weeks after their return from Frankfurt when Kate decided it was time to go. That she should cut her contract short and leave Preston Aviation while she still could, before she made a complete fool of herself once again, and fell in love.

Now all she had to do was tell Saul, which, since she'd been doing her utmost to avoid him since they'd got back, was easier said than done. It wasn't until Friday evening that Kate finally plucked up the courage to go through with it.

"Just knock and go in," June, his secretary, suggested, seeing her hesitate outside the doors to his suite. "He's in a good mood, so don't worry. Just gone and bought himself the perfect home, so if you've got something to ask him, you couldn't have picked a better moment."

Thanking June for her usual insight into their employer's state of mind, Kate followed her advice and knocked.

Saul was seated at his desk, preoccupied with the screen of his laptop. "Kate?" He glanced up as she entered. "What a pleasant surprise. I thought you'd already left for the weekend. This saves me having to phone you at home." Standing up, he gestured towards a seat just in front of him.

"I'd rather stand. Thank you."

"Oh?"

Holding her hands tightly in front of her to prevent them from shaking, she looked directly at him. "I've come to tell you I'm leaving – the company."

Her news appeared temporarily to knock him off balance. "You've come to do what?" he repeated blankly.

"Leave. It shouldn't really come as a surprise, since you've concluded the deal on the A320. Any more correspondence from Germany could always be sent—"

"The hell it will." He flung his pen down on his desk before turning his back on her, and striding towards the window. Picking up the catch, he flung it open.

"So this is how you repay me, is it?" he said, swinging round to face her. "Why you've spent most of your time avoiding me, since we got back from Frankfurt – you've gone and got yourself another job?"

Kate could feel her pulse race, her knees weaken, but she would not be shouted at. "I didn't...haven't got another job. I just thought you, of all people, wouldn't want someone working for you who isn't needed. I've even spent the last few days helping out in the accounts department!"

"So what are you complaining about?"

"I'm not an accountant, Saul, and I don't want to be, I'm a translator. I want to use my language skills."

"Even if it means leaving me?"

Kate looked up at him, puzzled, her heart hammering louder and louder against her ribcage. What did he mean by that?

"When we were in Germany, on that last night...when we were together...when we danced. And then afterwards, when we said goodnight, I thought... I hoped... Well, I sure as hell didn't expect this." He moved away from the window, allowing the cool breeze of evening to waft around the room.

Involuntarily, Kate shivered. "When we were in Germany," she reminded him as calmly as she could, "you rescued me from a couple of drunks and I was grateful."

"Grateful?" He threw the word right back at her. "Is that what you felt?"

No, that wasn't what she'd felt. Once she'd recovered from the shock of being accosted by a group of strangers, she'd enjoyed every minute of the evening with her rescuer. How could she tell him that, though? What future was there in it – in continuing with the relationship, once they were back? He was the owner of a multi-million pound company, who could go anywhere and get anyone. They didn't marry the likes of her. The Kate Fentons of this world were flirted with, slept with and then discarded. And she didn't want that. She deserved better.

"You haven't answered me. Is that what you felt – just gratitude? When I held you in my arms? When I...we kissed goodnight?"

"I... I don't see why we need to discuss this! Whatever I felt is not important. It could never be, because of who we are."

"And who are we, Kate?"

"I'm... I'm not prepared to discuss this further," she informed him, hoping her body wouldn't deceive her, and collapse in a pathetic little heap at his feet. "I'm going now. Perhaps we can discuss this on—"

"No, we bloody well can't. You'll stay and we'll discuss this now." Grabbing the phone, he told June to hold all further calls, and if she wanted to go home, that would be an excellent idea. "Now it's just us, Kate, you and me. And neither of us is leaving this room until we've sorted this mess out."

*

Kate opened her eyes. She was still alone. It was after two in the morning, and the chirrup of the cicadas in the fields below were her only companions. He wouldn't be back until at least four, she surmised, and then maybe even later. She pulled the sheet up and over her shoulders. It was chilly but she was too lazy to get up and find the control for the air conditioning, her mind drifting back to that night in Saul's office.

It had been chilly back then too, but Kate didn't dare suggest he close the window. For a few minutes she didn't even dare move. Then, as he obviously wasn't going to allow her to leave voluntarily, she took up his original offer of a chair.

"You can't keep me here all evening, Saul," she said sitting down. "I'm supposed to be meeting someone at eight and I don't want to be late."

"He can wait," he declared, taking up his usual position, perching on the edge of his desk just in front of her. "I suppose it is a he?"

Kate nodded.

"Do you want to phone him?"

She shook her head, wondering whether he could see through her deceit, or if Lydia was safe in her current guise as Kate's mystery man.

Saul, though, seemed to have lost interest. "What did you mean," he said, focusing on his previous question, "when you said it was not important because of who we are?"

"I... I did enjoy that evening in Germany. But..." She stopped, wishing he would move a little further away from her. How could she concentrate with him glowering down at her, cross-examining her like that? The force of his questions, of his voice, of his whole physique was almost unbearable. She wanted to shrink away from him, to put some distance between them. Then maybe he wouldn't be confusing her, causing her own body to strangle all rational thought. "You were kind to me," she said, trying to brave this heady potency, "and I was grateful."

"Oh God," Saul groaned, "there's that word again. I didn't do it because I wanted you to be grateful to me. If I'd wanted gratitude, I'd have rescued you, escorted you safely to your hotel room and said goodnight. Then you could have spent the rest of your life being grateful to me. I did it, you little fool, because I didn't want some drunk slobbering all over you, because I'd decided that if anyone was going to show you any sort of attention that night, it would be me."

Kate tried to suppress a sudden gasp. Had he just said what she thought he'd just said? "I don't understand."

"I told you on the plane going out that I wanted to spend some time with you. As usual, though, I'd got tied up in meetings, and every time I vowed to myself that I would ask you out, something got in the way. So you could say the drunks did me a favour. They made me forget business for a moment and play the conquering hero."

"I still really don't see what this has got to do with me leaving..."

Saul swung himself off the desk and placed his body right in front of her, the urgency of his presence completely overpowering her. She was trapped, and for the first time in her life, she didn't care. As though in a trance, she offered up her trembling hands. He swiftly enfolded them within his and pulled her up until she was swaying unsteadily in front of him.

"I don't want you to leave," he said, running his hands possessively along the length of her arms, "because I'm afraid I'll never see you again."

Bewildered, she gazed up as the corners of his mouth softened into a smile.

"Now do you understand what I'm trying to say?"

Kate nodded. "I think so." Then, remembering her earlier reservations, "I don't want to be one of your floozies."

He laughed. "Good God, whatever gave you that idea?"

When he could see that she didn't find the idea a laughing matter, he gently kissed her forehead, whispering, "I don't have floozies, as you call them. I've never had the time. I'll not lie to you, Kate, I've not led the life of a monk. I'm thirty-four, not thirteen, but you do me a gross insult if you think I'm the sort of man who indulges in fast women, or stupid women. I want an equal, my love, someone who will stand up to me when I'm being unreasonable, as I often am. Someone who's not afraid to tell me what they think. From the very first moment I saw you, in this very room, you stood your ground, insisting I was the one who had made the mistake, not the agency, nor June. Remember?" He placed his hands firmly on either side of her head, and tilted her face tenderly towards him. "I think I fell in love with you then."

"You did?"

"I did."

"I don't understand…"

"And there was I thinking that we understood each other

190

perfectly. I don't want a floozy, my darling, I want a wife. And not just any wife. I want you." He brushed her faltering lips with his, his dark eyes so full of unabashed longing that Kate thought that any moment she would squeeze her own eyes tight and wake up.

This was a dream, a wonderfully erotic dream, where Saul was proposing to her all over again. She was back in his office and he was there beside her, wrapping his arms, those strong, masculine arms, around her. Telling her he would never leave, that their love would last forever. How, if only she'd listened to him, that night in the gallery, if only she'd allowed him to explain, to dismiss what she saw, what she knew to be true, they could have been happy.

Kate nestled up to her pillow, to the warmth and the comfort, and she waited. She waited for something to happen, for Saul to rewrite history, but he never did. Her dreams were once again slowly slipping away from her, along with the night.

The alarm woke Kate with a start the following morning. It was seven thirty. Sunlight poured through the blinds and into the room, almost dazzling her with its ferocity. Blinking, she turned on to her side to see if Saul was up yet. To her surprise, it didn't appear as if he'd gone to bed. Or if he had, someone had remade the bed to look exactly as he'd left it last night, which led her to one conclusion and one conclusion only.

He hadn't come back last night. Sitting up, she grabbed her mobile and frantically scanned her messages. There were none, at least from Saul. But she didn't call him, didn't try to contact him, because she didn't need to. She knew exactly where he was. There was no accident. No car crash. No-one waiting to break bad news to her, to tell her of a tragedy. Oh no, the reason why he hadn't come back last night was simple, so simple that it tore at her heart with a dagger. He'd spent it with a redhead called Shelly Oppenshaw. Or should she call her Shel? Bitch, at the moment, seemed more appropriate.

And yet, Kate thought as she jumped out of bed, it took two to tango. However seductive the lovely Ms Oppenshaw might have been, she would never have enticed him into bed unless it was what he wanted. A dry tickle caught in her throat, as a pain, an all too familiar pain, rose up and greeted her with the ghosts of her past.

How could you? she wanted to scream, as she began to pace up and down. How could you do this to me again – after everything we've been through? After everything that's happened?

She paused as she reached the balcony. Flinging back the doors, she stepped outside. The heat hit her immediately from every direction. It was going to be another blisteringly hot day, but Kate didn't care. The beauty of the land around her, of the mountains as they mingled with the sky, the brilliance of the bougainvillaea and the sweet smell from the honeysuckle were all lost on her now.

She wanted to go home. To get back to work, to talk about deadlines with Lydia, to be asked out to the theatre by Tim, and to curl up in her pyjamas and eat sushi. But most of all, more than anything else, Kate wanted to go home and tell her mother just how wrong she'd been about Saul. And how she would never, ever, give her that opportunity again.

Chapter 16

Saul still couldn't understand how he'd allowed himself to be talked into sampling Majorca's exotic nightlife. One minute he was happily working on his redefinition of friendship, and the next he was sharing a taxi with a stranger, who was sidling up to him as though he were the last man left in the universe. Under other circumstances he might have been flattered, but Shelly wasn't Kate, and at that particular moment no-one else would suffice. If he couldn't have the woman he loved, he didn't want anyone.

On his way back to the hotel with Pete and his wife, several Spanish brandies later, he decided he had to put an end to this. First thing in the morning, he would tell Kate how he felt. How he really felt. How he really, really felt. He relaxed back against the torn upholstery of the taxi and smiled to himself. What was he – some kind of Spice Girl?

Any minute now he'd be breaking into song, which, unless he wanted an impromptu lesson in how to hitchhike Majorcan style, was not a good idea. The driver looked as though he'd been in the ring with Mike Tyson and won, which was more than Saul was currently capable of doing.

Tomorrow, though, things would be different. Tomorrow, Kate would finally understand why he'd let her go. Why he'd made no attempt to contact her during the past three years, to make her listen to what had really happened that night at the gallery. He should have done it sooner but he'd been too hurt. Too bloody hurt that she could think so little of him, that she could shut him out, without even giving him a chance to explain.

But now? Now Saul would go down on his knees and make a first-class fool of himself, if he had to. He didn't care. All he knew was that when – if – she walked out of his life tomorrow, she'd be saying goodbye to the man and not the myth.

It was after nine when Saul arrived back in their bedroom the following morning. A quick survey revealed all Kate's luggage neatly piled near the door. But no Kate. Her bed was clear of any trace of habitation and, as he peered into the bathroom, it looked as if she'd packed all her toiletries too.

"Kate?" He called out to her again, but there was still no answer. This did not bode well. What if, after all her reassurances to the contrary, her asthma had returned? What if she'd been rushed to hospital? Or worse?

He seized his mobile and dialled her number. Nothing. It went straight to voicemail. "Damn," he cursed as he grabbed the hotel phone and called reception. "Hello? Yes. I'm trying to locate Kate Fenton. Has a message been left for me – Saul Preston?" He waited, knowing the rest of his life could hinge on the answer to this one question. "No?" He slammed the receiver down. There was no time for pleasantries. His mind was whirling with possibilities.

If she wasn't in the breakfast room, and he hadn't seen her by the pool, or the terrace on his way up here, then where the hell was she?

Gathering up his keys, he was about to start an extensive search of the hotel when the balcony doors swung open behind him. There, with her long dark hair and flimsy cotton dress billowing in the gentle breeze from the mountains, stood the woman his imagination had catapulted into the next world.

"Kate, thank God!" Without hesitating, he strode towards her. All he wanted to do was to wrap her in his arms and keep her there. He didn't know when he'd been more pleased to see her. The only problem was that she didn't look quite so pleased to see him. "Has something happened?" He came to an abrupt halt. "Are you OK? Because you don't look it. Is it Helen? Don't tell me something's happened to your mother? Kate?"

"Did you have a good evening?"

"No, as a matter of fact I didn't, which is what I want to talk to you about." He broke off again. Something still wasn't right. "Will you stop looking at me like that, as though I'm something the cat brought in? I've already had two showers this morning: one to wake me up and one to make sure I stayed awake, so I know it can't be that."

"Why doesn't that surprise me?"

"What – that I've had two showers? Or that I needed waking up?"

"Was she worth it, Saul? The showers, I mean. Were you afraid that I would smell her perfume? That sickly odour of dead flowers?"

Saul took several steps backwards. "Hang on a minute. What are you talking about?"

"Shelly Oppenshaw, that's what I'm talking about. The woman you deserted me for at dinner. Remember? The one you sold our house to and then took on a tour of Majorca's nightclubs?"

It was as though the last three years hadn't happened. "Let me get this straight," he said, trying to keep calm. "You think I spent the night with Shelly? You do, don't you? You think I went out on a one-night stand and…and…" He couldn't bring himself to think the word, let alone say it.

"I don't think it," Kate said sadly. "I know it. And why do I know it? Because a leopard never changes his spots. He might disguise them slightly, but they're still there, under the camouflage."

"I don't believe this. After everything I've done to show you how I feel?" Saul raked his hands in anguish through his hair. He didn't know what else to do with them. "I didn't come back—"

"I don't want to know." Kate put her hands over her ears in desperation. "Please don't. I don't want to know."

But Saul wasn't listening. He picked up the phone.

"What are you doing?"

"I'm phoning reception."

"Why?"

"To speak to the manager. To get you to speak to the manager."

"But I don't want to speak to the manager."

"You will speak to the manager."

"No. No, I won't… I don't want to hear what he's got to say."

"Kate…" Saul could feel his throat dry up; perspiration begin to break out across his brow. "Speak to the manager. Please."

She collapsed on to her bed. "You're doing it again, aren't you? You're pushing me…"

"Pushing you? How the hell can I be pushing you? All I want is for you to know the truth." Carefully he lowered the receiver. "But you don't want to know the truth, do you?" The blood drained from his face. "You never do, do you? It wouldn't matter what I said, because your mind's made up, isn't it? Just like last time. And of course, you're always right." He broke off, aware that he was beginning to sound bitter, and Saul didn't want to sound bitter. He was going to get through the next few minutes with something called dignity if it was the last thing he did.

"I came here this morning to tell you that, despite everything we've been through, I didn't want us to part, that I couldn't be content with just being friends. But I can see now I would be wasting my time. No." He put out his hand to silence her, conscious that it was shaking more than he would have wished. "Don't say anything. I don't want to hear it. Not now. I want you to leave. Do you hear me? I want you to go. I'll... I'll meet you in reception. After I've packed."

Then, when she hesitated, when she sat looking straight back up at him, with such hurt indignation in those large green eyes, he could stand it no longer.

"For Christ's sake, Kate. Please. Just go."

Chapter 17

After the first few weeks, life began to fall back into place for Kate, as she retreated into the security of Fenton and Butler Translations. This was her world, created by her, and managed by her. There was no place for unwelcome visitors and, with the amount of work coming in, no time to think. It was just what Kate needed, what she had to have, if she were to survive. A world in which there was no time to think about him.

Only it wasn't the panacea she'd hoped it would be. As the languid days of summer faded into those of autumn, Kate soon found that her heart wasn't the only thing to be affected by Saul's absence. Something strange was happening to the rest of her. At first she put it down to some curious side effect of her erratic eating, assuming that her body was devising some secret plan of its own to protect itself against the oncoming winter. Of course, Kate knew this was nonsense. How could it be anything else? It was, however, a far more preferable alternative to her other theory, which was disturbing her sleep, her concentration at work, and making her snap at everyone.

"That's it," Lydia declared, as September became October.

"I can stand this no longer. I watched as you flung yourself back into your work after Majorca and said nothing. I thought, let her get it out of her system. When she's ready she'll talk to me, like in the old days. Do you remember the old days, Kate? When we used to go clubbing together? When we used to confide in each other?"

Kate watched from the safety of her desk, wondering exactly what it was that had upset Lydia so much. "Have I said something to offend you?"

"Not exactly. Not in so many words, but you're becoming impossible to work with. We never know which way you're going to jump next. You even yelled at poor Tim yesterday because he'd put too much milk in your tea."

"It made me feel ill," Kate muttered, wondering why now, after all those months of lying in bed, dry-eyed, desperate to expel Saul's ghost from her mind, she wanted to collapse in a heap and sob. Not a gentle sob either, but a heartfelt bawl, which would probably be heard within a five-mile radius. She swallowed quickly. "I'm sorry," she said, praying the moment would pass. "Truly I am. I know I've been difficult. I do, honestly, it's just…"

"Just what? I know Majorca was a disaster, but it's over. And I know he's a bastard." Lydia paused. "At least, I assume he's a bastard as he's made you so unhappy again, but you do have us, you know. Tim and I want to help. At the risk of sounding corny, that's what friends are there for, you idiot."

Kate pulled a tissue from the box on her desk and tried to blow her nose. "That was a lovely speech. And you're a wonderful friend. So is Tim. And if I thought you could help me through this, I would tell you. But no-one can help me at the moment."

"Don't be silly, of course we can."

Kate raised her eyes to meet her friend's. "No, you can't. You see, I think… No, I know I'm pregnant."

It was raining the following evening when the intercom went, and Kate discovered her mother standing on the front steps of her building, sheltering under an enormous umbrella.

"Mum?" she queried, as calmly as she could. "What are you doing here?"

"Just thought I'd say hello."

"Wouldn't it have been cheaper to have phoned?"

"Could you let me in, dear?" Helen countered. "Only I'm starting to get some funny looks from people down here."

"Sorry." Kate pressed the button and waited. She wished she'd known her mother was coming, then she could at least have tidied up a bit, or restocked the fridge. Now she would have to listen to the inevitable. The 'no wonder there's nothing of you' speech as Helen did her usual inspection, and despaired at the lack of contents.

Kate patted her expanding waistline. Well, that was one thing her mother couldn't say tonight. Tonight her daughter's eating habits would be the least of her worries. What on earth was she doing in London? And why, after having confided in Lydia yesterday, wasn't Kate surprised to see her?

"There I was," Helen began, as Kate helped her off with her raincoat, "wondering what to do for the weekend, and suddenly I had this wonderful idea: I would go and see my daughter. After all, we've hardly had a chance to have a really good chat since you came back from Majorca."

Kate gave her mother a warm hug. "I suppose Lydia sent for you."

"Lydia? No. Why, should she?"

Kate was unconvinced, but decided to let the matter rest. What did it matter who'd sent for Helen? The fact was she was here, and for the first time in years, Kate was glad. She really did need her mother. She was in danger of losing her way, and there was no-one better qualified to reroute her than someone who'd spent a lifetime telling her which path to follow, only to be wilfully ignored.

Even so, she couldn't tell her immediately. It wasn't something you could just blurt out to an unsuspecting grandma-to-be. She had to lead up to it gradually.

"Mum," she began, stretching out on the sofa after one too many sweet-and-sour chicken balls, "there's something I've got to tell you, and I don't want you to say anything until I've finished, OK?"

Helen looked up from trying to do *The Times* crossword. "Don't tell me you and Tim are engaged? Please, Kate, don't tell me that."

Kate struggled to keep a straight face. "No, Tim and I are not engaged, although that's not such a bad idea."

"Katherine!"

"It's all right." She smiled. "You can rest assured. I am not about to marry Tim, or anyone else, come to that. No," she said, taking a deep breath and crossing everything she could think of, "I'm pregnant."

Helen didn't say a word.

"I know I should have told you before," Kate continued quickly, surprised at the silence, "but I wasn't sure. My periods have been erratic for the last year because of my crazy eating habits, and I've not been feeling sick. Apart, that is, from when someone puts too much milk in my tea, or I smell that lavender air freshener, but that's all. And we did take precautions, before you ask. The rubber must have perished or something." She paused. "Are you shocked?"

"Shocked? Oh, no, oh my dear, no, I'm not shocked." Helen peered at her over her horn-rimmed glasses. "What I want to know is, who's the father?" This was the part Kate had been dreading, the part when her mother would resurrect her Cheshire cat act. "It's Saul, isn't it?" Kate could almost see that saucer of cream. "Have you told him?"

"Of course not."

"Oh, but you must, darling, you simply must tell him."

"Why? This is the twenty-first century. We were emancipated in the last century, in case you hadn't noticed. I don't need a man in order to bring up a child. I have my own business, with Lydia. I have money and friends."

She paused over this last word, mentally rehearsing what she was going to say to one friend in particular on Monday morning. Seeing her mother was one thing, but listening to her plead for Saul's part in this blissfully independent life Kate had just described was another thing altogether.

"And I don't want you going behind my back and telling him," Kate said quickly, before Helen could formulate a plan to do just that. "Do you hear me? You have to promise me you won't tell him."

"But that's just it, my dear. I don't know if I can. Promise you, that is."

"Why ever not?" Kate repeated, scarcely able to believe her ears. She knew her mother liked Saul, that she still saw him, but to betray her own daughter – over something as important as this? "Mum, please!"

"All right, all right," Helen said soothingly. She eased herself out of the armchair and went to where Kate was sitting. "Stop worrying," she said, sitting down and giving her daughter a hug. "Of course I won't tell him, if it's that important to you, I promise," she added, clasping her daughter's hands in hers.

"Thank God for that."

"But that now means I have to break a promise in order to keep one. It's no good, but I can't go to my grave without telling you what I know. Perhaps I should have done it earlier, but I gave him my word."

Kate gulped. "Him?"

"When you came back from Majorca, and told me what a rat he'd been, I couldn't believe it. I didn't want to believe it. As you say, I can be a stupid, romantic old fool, but I couldn't believe I could have been so wrong about him. So I went to see him."

"You did what?"

"I told him I was coming to London to meet your Auntie Hilary, who, by the way, has just got divorced from husband number four. Anyway, he met me and we went out to a very nice little restaurant, and I had it out with him there and then. I demanded to know what had happened."

"Oh, Mum," Kate groaned, trying to blot out the visual image which her mother had just conjured up so effectively.

"He went very quiet. And then he made me promise, in

no uncertain terms, that if he told me what had happened that night in Majorca, I must never tell you. Now do you see what my problem is?"

Kate jumped up and started to pace the floor. "But I don't want to know what happened that night. For God's sake, Mum, I *know* what happened that night. He slept with Shelly Oppenshaw. On the same day as he sold our home to them, he slept with the sister of the new owner. Have you any idea how much that hurts? That I'm carrying his child? And that I still love him?" It was out before she could stop herself, and now it had been voiced, there was no going back. No more pretence.

She stopped and stared out of the window. So much had happened since the night of Maria's wedding, when she'd stood in this room and asked herself over and over again why he'd kissed her. Now, deep down inside, she held something far more precious than a kiss. She held life itself. And he'd made it possible.

"Do you really love him?" Helen asked.

"I love him so much it hurts, and I don't know how to stop it," she said, resting her hands against the warmth from the radiator. "Every time I think about it, of what's happened, I think of him and wish he were here with me. But he's not and I've just got to learn how to get on without him. I've done it before, and I can do it again."

"Oh, my dear, if you would only take time to think for a moment. To stop being so fiercely independent. Of course, I blame myself for all of this, myself and your father. If we hadn't been so happy together, then maybe you wouldn't constantly be seeking perfection."

"I'm not seeking perfection."

"Aren't you? Then why do you always run at the first sign of trouble? That poor boy at school, who only wanted to say sorry. And then there was that chap at uni, who kept sending you flowers..."

"He cheated on me. They both cheated on me."

"And Saul – what about Saul?"

Kate blinked back tears. "He doesn't want me either, Mum, at least not in exclusivity."

Helen looked at her daughter sadly. "It's no good," she said finally. "Saul may hate me for what I'm about to do, but I would hate myself more if I didn't. And what you decide to do with the knowledge is up to you, my dear. All I ask is that you listen to your heart. For the first time in your life, Katherine, stop being afraid of being hurt, and listen to your heart."

Chapter 18

When Kate's official invitation to the preview of Alicia Gonzalez's exhibition arrived a few weeks later, she at last had the excuse she needed to visit the gallery.

She'd mulled over what her mother had told her, examining it over and over again. She'd gone to bed thinking about it, and woken up from dreaming about it. And the result was always the same. Saul was innocent. He was innocent of every infidelity of which she'd accused him. And what made it worse was that it hadn't come as a surprise. It was as though Kate had always known he would be, that Saul would never have been capable of the crimes of which he'd been accused.

His only crime had been to love her. And she'd punished him shamefully for that offence, over and over again.

He hadn't spent the night with the glamorous redhead from Texas. Every time Kate recalled her mother's words, she wanted the ground to open up and devour her. He'd left the Oppenshaws raving the night away in Palma, and returned to the hotel with Pete and his wife just after four in the morning. Knowing that there was no way he could share the room with Kate, feeling as amorous as he did, he'd secured the use of a couch in the manager's office.

According to Helen, Saul and the manager had struck up an unlikely friendship during those few days, and on that particular morning, the manager and anyone else who was passing had been treated to an especially moving rendition of a poem by Elizabeth Barrett Browning, followed by a brief monologue on what a bloody fool he'd been.

This had been cut short, apparently, by one of the guests. She hadn't understood a word of it, but the delivery had been so poignant she'd burst into tears. Saul had spent the next five minutes with his arm around the elderly lady, assuring her that it was all right, that *he* was all right, because he was going to sort things out. First thing tomorrow morning. He would lay his heart on the line. And this time Kate would listen to him.

And that, swore Helen, was the truth. She could see no reason to disbelieve Saul. He had enough alibis to litter a courtroom, so what could he possibly achieve by lying to her? He'd also sworn her to secrecy and he knew that her word was her bond. Helen took matters of confidence very seriously, just as she had the last time he'd confided in her.

Kate's ears had pricked up at that stage. "What last time?"

"Ah." Helen shifted awkwardly in her seat. "Now, I don't want you to get cross about this, dear, but I did promise you I would tell you everything."

Kate groaned. She wasn't sure she liked the word 'everything'. "Could you forget I asked the last question? I'm not sure I want to hear anything else." She was still reeling from the first piece of news.

"That's just the point, though, isn't it, dear? You don't want to hear what I've got to say because you've closed your ears to the truth. To the fact that you might, just might, be wrong."

"That's not true…"

"Isn't it? Darling, I can say these things because I'm your mother. And I want you to know that Saul has never knowingly hurt you."

"I suppose you're now going to tell me that what I saw that night at the gallery was a figment of my imagination? That I didn't see that woman rush past me with her breasts hanging out?"

"No, I'm not going to tell you that, because it wasn't a figment of your imagination. But there was a perfectly innocent explanation, as he tried to explain to you at the time."

"I don't want to know. Do you hear me?" Kate said, jumping out of her chair. "I don't want to know."

"Katherine, calm down, else you'll upset the baby."

"Upset the baby? What about me?" she cried, not knowing which way to turn. "Oh, Mother, I don't think I'm strong enough for this…"

"Of course you are, my darling. You have to be. Now, I know you think I'm always taking his side. But I'm not. I only have your best interests at heart. And I'd never have spoken to him about that night if I hadn't seen an article in one of the tabloids just over a year ago."

Kate stopped pacing. She knew she was going to regret this, but she had to ask. "What article?"

"If you'll stop moving around the room as though you're in training for the next Olympics, I'll tell you."

"Sorry." Kate came to an abrupt halt and sat back down.

"That's better," Helen said soothingly. "Where was I? Oh, yes, I was wrapping up some china for the church bring-and-buy sale, when I noticed an article about the forthcoming marriage of the Honourable Claudia Faux-Powell to Lord Wilcoxin. Well, naturally, I read it, and you can imagine my surprise when I saw that the bride-to-be had been undergoing rehabilitation for drug addiction. Apparently she'd been battling against this addiction for over *five* years!"

Why did her mother have to put quite so much emphasis on the number five? Kate wasn't stupid and she knew exactly where Helen was leading with this story. She just wasn't sure she wanted to hear it. "Do you want a cup of coffee?" she asked, springing back up.

Helen followed her daughter into the kitchen. "I'll help you make it, and while I'm here, I'll tell you the rest of the story. How, when Saul popped in to see me, earlier this year, I asked him about all of this."

Kate almost dropped the coffee jar. "You did what?"

"I asked him why he'd hired someone who was on drugs, and whether he'd known about it before he'd hired her."

"What...what did he say?"

"Nothing at first. You know what he's like, hates talking about personal matters. But after a lot of persuasion and one or two glasses of Mr Pearson's excellent homemade wine, he told me what he'd tried to tell you that evening at the gallery. How he was helping an old friend of the family's who was at his wits' end to know what to do with his daughter. Fortunately for Saul, or so he thought, his assistant was just leaving, so he came up with the brilliant idea of offering Claudia a job." Helen paused and looked in the fridge. "Where do you keep your milk?"

"I don't think I've got any."

"No problem, I'll have my coffee black. Now, where was I? Oh, yes, Saul's brilliant idea. Well, it didn't work. Claudia became more infatuated with her employer than with the job, but he couldn't sack her because of her father. On that particular night in August, when you saw her coming out of the gallery, she was as high as a kite. She'd come to see him, determined to have him – or whatever it is that you young people call it."

Kate handed her mother her drink, wishing that she'd get to the point. "And?" she prompted helpfully.

"And he rejected her. She then became hysterical and started to rip her clothes off to try and arouse him. And that's when you came in, my darling, and turned his whole life upside down."

"*I* turned *his* life upside down?"

"You never gave him a chance. When he tried to tell you, you refused to listen."

"I was having an asthma attack."

"Katherine. Please, I'm your mother. You refused to listen. You always do. And worse still, you sent him away."

Kate felt wretched. "I didn't know."

"He tried to explain."

"I know. I know. And I wouldn't listen. And then, at the hotel, I wouldn't listen again. Oh, Mother," Kate moaned, tears welling up in her eyes. "I've been such a fool. Such a stupid fool. And now he doesn't want me."

"I wouldn't say that," Helen said softly.

Kate glanced up. "When you saw him the other month?"

"You've hurt him, my dear, and at this moment I'm sure he wouldn't care if he never saw you again. But I've seen that look before. Three years ago. And he still came back for more."

Kate threw herself down on the stool in despair. "I can't wait another three years," she groaned, "I just can't."

"Then go to him. Tell him how you feel. Beg him for forgiveness."

"And then?"

Helen smiled. "And then, my dear, the rest is up to you."

Kate stared up at the entrance to Grenville Fine Arts. She was standing on the edge of a precipice. If she got it wrong this time, there would never be another chance, for any of them.

"Excuse me," she said, trying to attract the attention of Mandy at the desk, whose nose was firmly buried in Kafka's *The Metamorphosis*, "but is Saul Preston here?"

Mandy looked up and shook her head. "You're the woman in the picture, aren't you?" She peered at Kate intently over a pair of designer glasses. "I thought you were when I saw you last time, but I wasn't sure."

Kate raised her eyebrows in surprise. "What picture?"

"The one in the study. Look, I'll show you." And before Kate knew what was happening, she found herself in a room at the back of the building. There, surrounded by art in frames and art unframed, books on shelves and in piles on the floor, hung the picture in question. It was an oil painting of herself, her large green eyes sparkling as though she'd just heard an amusing anecdote.

So, he'd had the portrait commissioned after all, from the

sketches they'd approved. And he'd hung it here where he could see it. Day after day, week after week, and year after year. Her soul ached for the man behind the gesture. If that wasn't love, she didn't know what was.

"Thank you, Mandy. That will be all."

Kate spun round, all nostalgia calcifying in the austerity of those words. This was going to be more difficult than even she'd anticipated. As she noticed the familiar restraint mask every feature of that well-loved face, impossible might have been a more suitable word.

"You look tired." It was the first thing she could think of to say to him, but it came straight from the heart.

"I've just had a five-hour meeting."

"I'll get you a cup of coffee," Mandy said, before turning towards Kate on her way out. "Would you like a drink, Ms...?"

"Miss Fenton will not be staying long enough, thank you, Mandy. I'll have mine black and strong, but leave it in the kitchen. I'll collect it in a minute. In other words," he added, his tone softening, "could you give us a few minutes alone please?"

Kate had never seen anyone disappear so quickly. Perhaps in a past life Mandy had been a magician's assistant. Either that or Saul had been taking conjuring lessons. Of one thing Kate was certain, though: he would not get rid of her quite so easily.

"I didn't realise that you'd had my painting finished," she said, clutching at the back of the chair behind his desk for support. "That you've still kept it. Thank you."

"What for?" His voice was dismissive. "I only kept it because it's a damned good painting."

Why did he have to say it like that? As though she didn't mean anything to him?

"Look, Kate, I don't know why you've come here this afternoon, but whatever it is, I don't have time for it." He glanced down abruptly at his watch. "I'm already running late for my next meeting. And then I'm supposed to be going out tonight. So if you've got something to say, say it, and then please leave."

"I wanted to thank you for the invitation...for still using me as Alicia's interpreter."

"You could have phoned. Left a message with Mandy, or emailed me. That wasn't why you came. And I really haven't got time to play guessing games." His eyes searched her face. She could feel herself begin to blush. "You're looking well," he said, after a few seconds.

"I am, but not for the reasons which I suspect are whizzing through your mind. Would you mind if I sat down?" Without realising it, she had been applying all her tension into the back of that leather upholstery, and she wasn't sure how much more either she or the chair could take. "No? Never mind. Looks like I'll have to stand, then." She took a deep breath. "I wanted to apologise. To say sorry."

"I know what apologise means," he informed her bluntly. "Now you've apologised, you can go."

"Saul, you didn't hear me," she said, trying to stay calm. "I said I was sorry."

"You're wrong, Kate. I heard you. Your mistake is thinking I care."

There was to be no unbending here, no softening of any kind.

This was not good. Not good at all. But she had to be strong. Deep within her lay a little miracle in which he'd played a major role, and for all their sakes, she had to be strong.

"Don't you want to know why I'm apologising, or what I'm apologising for?"

"No."

"Well, I'll tell you then…"

"No, you damned well won't."

And with those words all attempts at self-restraint vanished. Before she knew what was happening, she'd been seized by the wrists.

"Saul," she said, struggling to free herself from his grip, "I need to talk to you."

"You're not listening to me, are you?" he said, as she found herself with her back up against the wall, the breadth of his body blocking any chance of escape. "You never listen, do you? You didn't listen to me that night in the gallery, you didn't listen to me at the hotel and you're not listening to me now. I said I wasn't interested."

She could feel his breath, warm and sensual, breaking in torrents against her face, her eyes transfixed by the sudden flare of passion in his.

"Why have you come here today, Kate? What have you really come for? What gives you the right to…to walk in here just when you feel like it, without…without any warning… Christ!"

And for a second, as the imprint of his fingers dug a little deeper into her arms, and his mouth seemed to almost brush past her lips, she thought he was going to kiss her, that he was going to show her just how inadequate words were at moments like these. But he didn't. Instead he released her and, almost pushing her from him, turned to move away.

Quickly catching hold of his sleeve, she tried again. "Saul..."

He shook himself free. "Does this give you pleasure?" he asked, rounding on her, the pain in his voice cutting her to the quick. "Does this turn you on?

"No. No, of course not. *You* turn me on, though."

"Kate, please..."

"You turn me on so much at times it scares me."

Saul didn't answer. He appeared lost for words, but as Kate saw him swallow hard, she knew it was more than that, much more than that.

"I love you," she said softly. "I wouldn't blame you if you don't still love me. I'm not the easiest person to love. And I wouldn't blame you if you still threw me out, if you flung me over your shoulder and chucked me outside on to the pavement. Only, could you make sure that I had a soft landing?"

She held her breath.

"A soft landing?" he repeated numbly.

"Only if you're thinking of dumping me somewhere, that is. It's just that I'm a little particular at the moment about where I'm thrown."

"And...and you want a soft landing?"

"Yes. Please."

He cleared his throat. "There's only one place around here with a soft landing."

"And where exactly would that be?"

"Upstairs."

"Upstairs as in your flat?"

Saul gave the merest hint of a nod, and for the first time since she'd walked through that door, Kate allowed herself to hope. "You wouldn't be talking about your bed now, would you?" she queried quietly.

The nod was a little more pronounced. As was the gentle tilt of his mouth.

"And this bed, is it currently unoccupied?"

"Do you mean have I got someone in it, warming it for me? No, it's quite empty."

"That's good then, isn't it?"

"Is it, Kate? I don't understand what's happening here. I don't understand what's happening here at all."

"Why don't you cancel your next meeting then, and let me explain?"

Several weeks later and Saul was bloody glad he had. He was standing in the middle of an ultrasound department, while the woman he loved was lying outstretched on an examination couch before him; her gown pulled up so that it was resting just above her navel, her stomach a sticky mess of jelly. And she had never looked so happy or so beautiful.

"That's ours," Kate whispered, as an image of their baby flashed up before them on the screen. "Isn't she wonderful?" Her fingers linked tightly through his.

Saul couldn't answer. He was having difficulty finding the words to express what he was feeling. And now was not the time to break down and make a total prat of himself. So, instead, he just squeezed her hand a little tighter, and wondered how Kate could tell from the image that their creation was going to be female. He was obviously not looking in the right places!

Later that evening, as Kate stood reflecting on the day's events in front of their bedroom mirror, Saul came up behind her and gave her a hug. Snuggling back against his chest, she smiled at his reflection in the glass.

"I'm glad you didn't sell this house," she said. "I'm sorry that it upset Mr Oppenshaw so much that he threatened to sue you, but I'm glad it's still ours."

Gliding his hand protectively over Kate's rounded stomach, he kissed the top of her hair affectionately. "Do you know what I was thinking this afternoon at the hospital?"

Kate shook her head. "No, but I've got a feeling you're going to tell me."

"I was thinking how close I came to losing all of this. You and the baby. That if you hadn't come to the gallery that afternoon, I might never have known."

"I would have brought Alicia to your opening next month, as promised. I think even you would have noticed my slightly extended waistline!"

"But then it would have been too late. You would have refused to marry me because you would have thought I was only interested in the baby."

Gently Kate lifted his fingers from her body, and swivelled round so that she could look him squarely in the eye. "If anyone's to blame, it's me. I was so scared of being hurt again that I never gave you a chance to explain, to dispel what I thought I already knew. That there's no such thing as perfection, at least not for me."

Gathering her up into his arms, Saul carried her towards their bed. "I am probably the most imperfect human being to have a perfect relationship with," he informed her, laying her carefully on the sheets, "but I swear I'll try and do better." Pulling his shirt free from the confines of his trousers, he began to undo the buttons. "And I will start by promising never to go clubbing with prospective house purchasers."

"Or their sisters."

"Especially their sisters. And I won't employ women with addictive personalities," he continued, wrestling with one defiant cuff button, "just because their father was a friend of my old man's."

Kate smiled mischievously. "If you do, you must tell me, and not keep it secret, so I don't get confused. So when I interrupt what looks like some sort of perverted sexual act between my fiancé and his assistant, looking as though she's been mauled by a lion, I won't jump to the wrong conclusion. Poor Claudia. I do hope she finally finds happiness with Lord whatever his name was."

"Lord Wilcoxin," Saul supplied, flinging his blue shirt on to the chair, and resting on the edge of the mattress to begin taking off his shoes and socks.

Kate leant across, allowing her fingers to run sensually up and down the muscular ridges of his back, tracing various paths amongst the warmth of his body. "And we won't mention Patti with the long legs, shall we, who just happened to belong to someone else?"

Saul groaned at the recollection. "Don't remind me."

"I'll try not to," she teased, affectionately. "And I won't invent boyfriends who don't exist just because I'm scared of committing to anything with one of the most aggressively wonderful men in the universe."

"Only *one* of the most aggressively wonderful men?" Saul queried. Having flung his shoes across the floor, he had climbed on to the bed, and was now on all fours as though he were about to pounce on her.

"*The* most aggressively wonderful man," Kate muttered quickly, trying to quell a little giggle. "Haven't you forgotten something? You're still wearing your trousers."

"I thought you might like to take those off for me, my darling. But before you do, I want you to answer me one thing."

"Anything," gasped Kate.

"And I want you to look at me when you answer this."

Dragging her attention away from his thighs, Kate gazed up into eyes so full of love that she wondered how she could ever have been so blind. If her mother hadn't intervened, dear, sweet Helen, none of this would be happening. But Saul would never know that. It would be a secret between mother and daughter, which Kate would take with her to the grave.

"Right, father of my unborn child, what is it that is so important that it cannot wait just a little while longer?"

"I want you to promise me one thing. I want you to promise that you will never, and I mean never, leave me. That next week, when you are asked to say, 'I do', your 'I do' will last forever."

Keeping her eyes firmly fixed on his, Kate delicately started to untie the little lace bows at the front of her slip, bow by bow, the silken material slipping away with each release.

"To have and to hold," she murmured, allowing one strap to slide invitingly from her shoulder. "From this day forward." The other strap fell enticingly away without any persuasion. "For better and for worse." With a little wriggle, the garment slithered down towards her waist. "For richer and for poorer."

Tentatively touching his flesh, her fingers began making little exploratory movements as they drew closer and closer towards his hips. "In sickness and in health." They paused fleetingly, before beginning to slowly undo the silver buckle of his belt.

"To love and to cherish." Teasingly, she gradually lowered the zipper. "'Til death do us part, I hereby plight thee my troth."

And somewhere across the moonlit room, resting on a volume of poetry by Elizabeth Barrett Browning, lay a black-and-white photograph. A poignant reminder of a life just beginning.

To find out more about Elly visit her website
www.ellyredding.com

Lightning Source UK Ltd.
Milton Keynes UK
UKHW010853080819
347620UK00002B/691/P